THE FACE THIEF

Also by Eli Gottlieb

Now You See Him
The Boy Who Went Away

THE FACE THIEF

Eli Gottlieb

WILLIAM MORROW
An Imprint of HarperCollins*Publishers*

HarperCollins books may be purchased for educational, business, or sales promotional use. For information please write: Special Markets Department, HarperCollins Publishers, 10 East 53rd Street, New York, NY 10022.

A hardcover edition of this book was published in 2012 by William Morrow, an imprint of HarperCollins Publishers.

FIRST WILLIAM MORROW PAPERBACK EDITION PUBLISHED 2013.

Designed by Diahann Sturge

Library of Congress Cataloging-in-Publication Data

Gottlieb, Eli.
   The face thief / Eli Gottlieb. — 1st ed.
      p.   cm.
   ISBN 978-0-06-173505-9
   1. Femmes fatales—Fiction.   2. Man-woman relationships—Fiction.
   3. Deception—Fiction.   4. Psychological fiction.   I. Title.
PS3557.O8313F33 2012
813'.54—dc22   2011025474

ISBN 978-0-06-173504-2 (pbk.)

13 14 15 16 17   OV/RRD   10 9 8 7 6 5 4 3 2 1

For my parents:

Leonard Gottlieb, 1917–2008
and
Esther Gottlieb, 1921–2010

CHAPTER ONE

Pain had a voice. It spoke to her as she shot off the top step and forward into space, patiently explaining that this was not how her life was supposed to end. It was supposed to end, the voice whispered, with her enjoying her dotage in some great British country house, filled with mullioned windows and about a mile of lawn. Or before a roaring fire of some kind, chilled gin in hand, witty remark at the ready. Returned afterward to her upstairs room, there'd be the littlest hiccup, the tiniest blip in the cardiac flow. And then she'd be lowered quietly and forever into distinguished oblivion.

A rhythmic pinging interrupted the daydream. It resembled the noise of someone counting change. Where was she having these thoughts, exactly? Were her eyes open or shut? She couldn't tell.

*Something awful was happening. She was certain of that. She was tumbling downward in what felt like slow motion while experiencing a terrible concussive series of blows to the head. These seemed a confirmation of sorts; the fit end to a long period of wondering what was going to happen next. **This** was going to happen next. A stair smashed into the orbital bone around her eye. Another one fractured a rib. She* *wanted to explain to someone that always, from childhood on, as a girl capering butterfly-bright around the house slung over Duxbury Bay, she'd had her realest conversations with books, with the endless piles of poetry and old novels whose characters moved with grave faces around the important questions of life, and that this, which was happening now, was something they would have* **certainly, thoroughly,** *and* **absolutely** *disapproved of.*

The next stair slammed into her upper forehead and opened up the skin, thereby causing a spray of arterial blood to darken the auburn hair once fingered by Joey Vandermere while they sat kissing in a car parked at Russian Hill below a bowl of summer stars, his voice soft in her ear as he whispered that college would soon draw each of them away into the far, cold reaches of the future, and in the meantime, did she love him long enough to let him unbutton her pants?

She continued standing and then falling, head over heels. The staircase seemed endless. And as she fell, she remembered not just Joey but all of them, a solemn procession of boys and then men, each of them taking his turn and passionately pleading his case. Many of them were married. These were invariably the most winsome in their appeal. Their self-adoring looks; their sly and roguish winks and grins: one of the things they had in common was the way each gave signs of "understanding" her, and of seeing her "special inner grace," even as they took their clothes off with their faces gone suddenly cold with sexual concentration.

Had she married one of them herself? Had she finally become more than that girl who still sat in her room, lifting her eyes again and again from her books, and looking into the onrushing dark of the future? Had she become famous and had children of her own?

She hit the ground floor hard, and as she lay there unmoving, she seemed to see as if down the barrel of a long lens to the cropped image of her childhood dog, Brandy, rearing up before her with its bright button eyes and its pink scrap of tongue. Then the lens pulled back to include the trees, homes, mountains and rivers around the dog, and then drew farther back in such a way that the earth slowly revealed itself to be a ball of clouds and blue water resting calmly on a palm of air. She continued to recede backward until the planet, eventually, winked out of sight in the dark immensity of space.

The pinging grew louder. She suddenly thought she understood. The pinging was coming from the large wooden metronome that had crouched on a shelf for the entirety of her childhood and spoken its clicking language as she sat playing her violin. Probably she was still a child, lying abed and dreaming she was an adult to whom terrible things had just happened. Probably, for that, she was just now coming home from school, rounding the corner at a tilt, zooming into the house with a breathy slam of the screen door behind her, and then up the stairs to where the violin lay in its case like a sleeping child. Tenderly she drew it out and placed her chin on the chin rest. She rosined her bow and pulled it along the strings. A clear voicelike note sang out. This was music. The metronome ticked like a single person applauding in an empty room. She was playing a Brahms composition. It was intensely sad and beautiful; it seemed as if the darkness were expressing itself. She played and played, while the metronome applauded, her bow leaped and wiggled on the strings, and the music mounted on a ladder into the air. The sound was imps and demons; it was gas become liquid and flowing upward, impossible. Then she was playing the fiendishly difficult "vivacissimo" passage with its triple stops and it was going perfect. This was a bursting-forth, a flowering of her. She drew from the instrument the last beautiful note and opened her eyes.

When her vision cleared, she saw several women standing before her. Were they angels? They had little pins on the whiteness of their *breasts and small boatlike white caps on their heads. One of them leaned forward. The ongoing pinging sound seemed to be calling something of terrible importance to order. It was coming from a white box on the wall by her bed. The angel gave a smile of pure forgiveness. Then, incredibly, the angel opened her mouth and said her name.*

CHAPTER TWO

He heard her before he could see her. He'd called for a volunteer from the audience and she emerged from the darkness like a woman out of a lake. Tall and slender, she somehow processed smoothly up the stairs toward him. Though she wasn't especially striking, he noticed right away that she carried herself with pure, complete confidence in her own attractiveness. She was as filled with it as a glass of milk is with white.

"Ladies and gentlemen, I'd like you to meet—"

"—Margot," she said, looking at him evenly.

"Margot," he relayed to the crowd through his microphone. "Margot," he said to her, "thanks for coming up onstage. We're going to get to you in a second." He turned again to face the audience of about sixty middle-level managers, unemployed salespeople, suspicious spouses and a smattering of New Agers. It was midmorning of his daylong seminar called *The Physique of Finance: The Art of Face Reading and Body Language for Professional Advantage.* His name was Lawrence Billings and he was fifty-three years old.

"In the meantime, a little check of our collective humors, everybody. As I already mentioned, we're gathered today for that most honorable of reasons: because we need a leg up. We've gathered because the life we knew as kids is now a big fat mess of dots and signals, and who among us doesn't feel a little snowed in by that digital blizzard? Remember the good old days of handshake contracts, folks? Remember signing documents with"—he made a slight grimace—"a *fountain pen*? Well, file all that under Extinct, and put it on the shelf by the Dodo, because it's never coming back!"

He'd started out his adult life as a classics major, had dropped that for the study of psychology, and over the course of it all spent twenty years polishing his innate sensitivities into something sellable.

"But the body," he said, "doesn't know a megabyte from a man on the moon. The body is continuing to tell its own simple truth about the person living in it, and if we can read that truth, we'll have an advantage even in a business climate as rushed, as strange, as flat-out bizarre as ours. Five hundred years from now, when a computer named President Tron lives in the White House, the body will remain the primary point of reference for that which makes us human."

As a child, he saw things. He had a diviner's gift for the hidden occult mysteries of ordinary life. Where other children saw an apple in a tree, he beheld a beating heart on a vine, intricately nourished by long, forking veins of green and eating dirt and sunshine to stay alive. Where they glimpsed a house on a patch of lawn, he saw an exploded box of wood and brick holding itself barely upright against the furious downward will of gravity. It was unclear to him why the moon didn't drop from the sky like a nickel coin or the people of the planet get thrown sideways into space like dust off a spinning top. The boring visible world shouted out loud with inner enigmas and adults were either in a conspiracy to pretend it wasn't so or were simply dumb.

"As Hamlet put it," he said resonantly, "'Like a whore, I unpack my heart with words.'" But then he immediately added in a normal speaking voice, "And did you know that seventy percent of the impression we make is nonverbal? And that on top of that"—he drew himself up—"the least reliable thing in this world is the information coming out of someone's mouth?"

Even as a boy, he'd understood the commonness of lying. People did it as naturally as singing. They simply slicked their hair back and belted out howlers, one after another. They held their heads subtly to the side by way of preparation. Then their eyes went all funny, a shot of trembly nerves went through their lips, and they lied. Parents did it to children. Children did it to siblings. Dogs did it to cats and cats to birds. And the TV did it to everybody, loudly, and all day long.

"A perfectionist," he said to the audience, "has more than two vertical lines between their eyebrows, true or false?"

"True," someone sang out.

"A big chin?" he asked.

"Gotta always be right."

"Straight eyebrows?"

"Linear thinker."

"Attached earlobes?"

"Commitment to family."

"All right"—he forced a laugh—"who's been looking at my notes?"

Attendance at his seminars had been declining steadily over the years, and in recent times a cold, whispering little wind of fear had begun to play at his back. Originally, at least a substantial portion of the crowd had been in it for kicks, party favors, recreational fun.

But over recent years the weakening economy had salted the room with fiftysomethings whose faces had about them the peculiar bleakness of formerly successful people now out of work and dazed by the recognition that help was probably not on the way.

"How about a gap between the front teeth?" he asked the audience.

There was a silence. Maybe that hadn't been in the breakfast handout.

"Risk taker, obviously," he said smoothly into his mike. The headset was slightly overamped; the sound boomed; he'd have to talk to the hotel manager about that.

"And speaking of risk," he said, "I'd like us to do a bit of live study with our lovely volunteer, Margot."

Their gazes crossed, and she stared at him a moment, smiling slightly while saying nothing back in return. Usually volunteers were unnaturally eager to please, and nervous, but this woman simply sat there, perfectly composed. Her hair was long and parted in the center, her eyes were strikingly large, green and alight; and she had a sense of calm containment about her, like someone waiting for a train.

"Go on," she said.

Staring at her, smiling back, he suddenly felt the Bump. The Bump was when the thing, the muscle, moved in the space under his solar plexus. A little sideways skip in his gut that was his special private way of signaling to himself that he was having a reaction, or better a Reaction, writ large. He saw dozens of people up close in a year. Of those, maybe half were women. Of those, only a handful were odd or interesting enough to snap him out of his reflex professionalism long enough to note their singularity. Every once in a while, he'd feel the slight shock of recognition of meeting someone genuinely compelling. The reasons for this were finally mysterious. By long-standing habit, he noted the Bump, and then buried it, deep.

"Please," he said to the crowd, "direct your attention to the video screens."

He busied himself for a moment in turning on a video camera, adjusting some small onstage lights, and then centering Margot's face in the camera. Her image, tremendously enlarged, appeared on the screens: big eyes, strong nose, thick, incurved lips.

"And here it is," he said, "the centerpiece of creation, the *locus classicus* of human feeling, the, ah, what I'm saying is, human face. Now normally, when we look at the faces of people we know, our looking is smudged all over with how we feel about them, good or bad. But what we have here"—he waved at the gigantic unsmiling face of Margot—"is a visage none of us have ever seen before, and that's a good place to start. More specifically, let's start at the top, with her hair."

He whipped out a small laser pointer and put a magnified dot on her forehead.

"Her hair is beautiful and rich. She looks like an out-of-work Breck girl. But what can we say about her hairline, eh?"

"S'where her hair begins?" a woman's voice sang out from one of the front rows.

"It's kinda jagged?" someone else asked.

"Bingo." He looked up into the darkness. "The hairline is like a graph of life during adolescence." He traced the laser dot along the ridges of her hairline. "And this jagged edge right here, well, that probably means our friend Margot's adolescence was less than smooth sailing, am I right?"

Just perceptibly, the corners of her mouth drooped as the shot went home. She looked directly into his eyes.

"You're right," she said, speaking intentionally loud enough to be picked up by the overhead mike. "Like many people I had a difficult, um, transition to adulthood."

He was still looking out into the darkness while savoring the moment when Margot leaned forward and, in a soft voice intended only for the two of them, asked, "Why do you seem to be enjoying this so much?"

After he sent her back to her seat, Lawrence spent the rest of the seminar subtly aware of her in his field of vision. Her tart rejoinder had surprised him, and out beyond the lights, where people were various piles and squibs of gray, he felt his eyesight snagging on the particular shadow he thought she was, and noting her, despite himself.

Smoothly, with a patter born of long practice, he led them through the Posture Circus, the Eyes Have It, and Mouthing Off. He did Right Face and Left Face, Feet First and All Hands Aboard, broke for lunch, and returned with his afternoon summaries: Bearing and Business, Voice and Value, and Finance and the Face.

He had mostly forgotten about the girl by the time the seminar concluded at five to a round of sustained applause and his appeal—done with fake bashfulness—to buy his book.

Fifteen minutes later, he was onstage packing up his notebooks when he felt her rising up the sides of his eyes. When he turned, she was standing in front of him, and to his surprise, he felt the Bump again; this time it wasn't in the solar plexus but near the liver.

"Hi there," he said.

She had small, close-to-the-head ears and an appealing aerodynamic skull that he hadn't noticed before. Below the level of body language, the actual structure of the body itself was a text, and he believed caches of readable data inhered in the way hips were fitted to pelvises; throats held the weight of the head; fingers tapered and skulls were shaped. A person was an endless manifest written over with the most intimate human information.

"Thank you," she said, "is what I want to say."

"Well, you're most welcome," he said, this time letting his eyes rest in hers in the "frontal social position."

"Margot Lassiter," she said, and held out her hand, flashing large green eyes at him.

"The first name I'd already gotten," he said, briefly shaking her hand.

He noticed that she was swaying, very slightly, as if hypnotized, on her feet. It was hard for him to square this suddenly bubbly open female with the reserved, suspicious woman he'd seen on-stage. As if she'd divined his thoughts, she said, "I know, sorry about that. You probably formed a pretty nasty first impression of me, didn't you?"

He actually laughed a moment, before catching himself.

"Nasty? Of course not," he said.

"I would have, in your shoes. But no hard feelings, I hope. You converted me," she said, and showed small white teeth to him in a smile, "over the course of the day. Can I call you Lawrence?"

"Sure."

She came a little bit closer.

"What it is," she said, "is I need work."

"Oh?"

"Drills, practice; I need to get up to speed as quickly as I can."

"Sounds pretty urgent."

"Well, it is, kind of. I have a business trip to the West Coast planned in a few weeks."

"Nothing replaces just sitting down and doing it. You've got the workbooks."

"Can I say something? I feel like a diner at a new restaurant with a menu of a thousand choices. It's all a bit, what, overwhelming."

"Can be," he said agreeably.

"And I totally intend," she said, "to do as you advised, and work on it a little bit each day, but uh . . ."

The slight weaving of her body, so subtle the average person wouldn't have noticed it, stopped on the spot. She seemed to grow slightly taller. Her voice had dropped at least six microtonalities to what, in his work, he sometimes called the range of the Insinuating General.

"Is it true you teach privates?" she asked.

Afterward—after she'd given him her card, told him she'd try to book an appointment with him via his website and chastely shaken his hand good-bye—Lawrence returned to his packing with a fresh thought in the forefront of his mind: she was a player! She had about her the bright, stylized artificiality of someone keeping up a front while angling for advantage. He shook his head to himself as he slid the microphone into its case. More often lately he was approached after seminars by middle-aged, somewhat defeated and usually out-of-work people who told him gamely he was helping them get "back on track." They often employed the vocabulary of recovery and had an air of deflated buoyancy about them. But players? People wanting to add this to their arsenal of deception who were already—because she was; he'd deduced this right away—gifted at self-concealment? That was something else entirely.

He finished packing in a hurry. He wanted to get out of the theater, out into the car, and back on the road where he could comfortably review the day. He was tired, as he always was by the end of a daylong seminar. He was lusting for his home, his gin and tonics and those dusk moments passed in his backyard with his wife in happy contemplation of nearby Hawk Mountain, where the rising tide of suburban development had stopped at last, defeated by the steepness of the slope, and left a lovely horn of green like a reference point of the dwindling natural world.

His house was an hour and a half away and, on impulse, he decided to stop for a quick drink first to refresh himself. He phoned his wife to tell her he'd be a little later than expected and then pulled over at one of his favorite roadside haunts, where he took a window seat and ordered his drink. Rush-hour traffic was thickening fast on the interstate, and as someone who spent about 150 days a year on the road, it was hard not to sometimes feel that the entire country was covered by the same whizzing, eye-level belt of noise and busyness.

His drink arrived, and as he sipped it, he took her card out and put it on the table.

Margot Lassiter, it read. *Editor at Large.* It then gave the name of a popular magazine. He studied the lettering and the design of the card for clues, contentedly chewing his ice. What was she after, exactly, and why the urgency to "get up to speed" before her "West Coast" trip? He'd already seen the hunger in her features; the chamfered lower lip indicating decisiveness; the slightly wolfish arrangement of the cheekbones and the prominent, take-no-prisoners chin. But it had been the watchfulness behind the eyes and the forced intonations of the voice that had alerted him to something in her that felt like cunning.

She posed a challenge—an interesting one in a season of contracting sales and rote presentations. But he was up to the challenge. And he was curious, as well. What was she finally after? He would find out soon enough, he thought, paying his bill and getting back into his car.

CHAPTER THREE

Three months later, in a small town in Northern California, a man named John Potash lurched awake with a convulsion as large as a sneeze, and shot out of a dream of careening forward motion and billowing fire back into his body. When he opened his eyes, the quiet of the room underlined his sensational mental violence. A leading edge of sun illuminated the thick carpet underfoot, touched the swirling colors of paintings hung on the wall, and lay most spectacularly of all on his wife, who was sprawled naked and asleep on the sheet next to him, her spine describing a long, lovely curve that seemed itself to symbolize the essence of trust.

He shut his eyes. From behind his lids he could feel the pinkish pressure of the sun, shining through his capillaries. It was the sun that was the problem. It was the blameless stupid illumination of the sun.

If not for the sun, and the languor it brought with it, he would almost certainly have let the phone ring through to voice mail when it buzzed alertly on the desk of his small rented office that day a few weeks ago. Instead, as a recent arrival in California, he'd shrugged off his (urban, Manhattan) suspicions on the spot, and stabbed "call" with his finger.

"Hello?"

"Mr. Potash?" A woman's voice, warm with a tone of rising complicity, was on the other end.

"Yes?"

"This is Janelle Styles of Greenleaf Financial. I hope you don't mind me calling you like this."

"Well, that depends," he said, hedging his voice in a way that could make his utterance either funny or sincere.

If not for the sun, he thought, getting quietly out of bed so as not to disturb his still-sleeping wife, he wouldn't have continued to banter with the woman, who seemed at every step of the conversation somehow a step ahead of his response. He entered the small frosted glass shower cubicle and turned the taps to cold, shivering under the freezing spray while the tape of the conversation, as it had every hour on the hour for several days, continued playing in his head with crisp, punitive fidelity.

"What it is, Mr. Potash," the woman was saying in memory, "is that Mr. Martin at the New York office personally forwarded me your name as someone who'd been an early investor in our Dyna-venture Fund and had already exited with an attractive return. I'm calling about a new, highly collateralized opportunity we feel *very* strongly about, and that we're offering exclusively to our best investors."

"Is that so?" he remembered saying, noncommittal.

"Yes. Now, normally, this type of investment wouldn't be available to someone like yourself, but Mr. Martin asked that you be allowed to participate alongside some very high net worth individuals and institutional investors because of how appreciative we are of the confidence you've shown in us in the past."

Potash squeezed the fragrant juice of shampoo onto his head and recalled that at this moment in the conversation there'd been a pause while he'd pondered her offer. He had first been introduced to Greenleaf Financial through two of the members of his home poker game in New York, each of whom had invested with positive results. Emboldened by their stories of excellent yields on wind farms and Mexican algae plantations, he was enticed to experimentally invest five thousand dollars. When his 11 percent returns were promptly deposited in his account, he doubled the amount. His next investment raised the bar still higher, to fifty thousand, with the same results. Greenleaf was not a hedge fund, nor an extravagant risk-taking operation based on funny-number math or cooked books. It was a consortium of forward-seeking investment advisers and analysts from elite business schools who roamed the world seeking the latest cutting-edge sustainable products. Predatory, cash-rich, not averse to opportunistic bottom-feeding, Greenleaf was masterful at saving companies teetering on the brink of bankruptcy, often snatching up extraordinary assets for ten cents on the dollar or less.

"Tell me more," he'd said to the woman.

Potash now leaned forward and turned the shower hot, then hotter still. It was as if he wanted to scald away the recollections, expunge the fluent bit of salesmanship that came next. Was he aware, he remembered her asking, of the new smartphone that boasted a bioplastic casing derived entirely from cornstarch, along with low-impact packaging and PVC-free electronics? Or how about hydrotreated renewable jet fuel to answer the need of an American aviation industry that was "sick of being the unwanted relative at the national petrochemical buffet"? If that wasn't enough, she added with a feathery, cascading downward chuckle, there were proton-exchange membranes in fuel cells, zinc-air batteries, and by the way, had he heard about the new Japanese experiment in organically growing a birch tree that was already treated, insect resistant and ready to be used as lumber?

Potash, at forty-two, had spent the majority of his adult life as the vice principal of a small alternative high school on the Upper West Side of Manhattan. His expertise was administrative; his gift was inspirational. Slim, affable, his face filled with the sympathetic curves of a born listener, he'd become the go-to guy for giving convincing speeches at fund-raising dinners, and could be counted on to provide a consoling shoulder for teachers caught in the hot cross fire between eruptive adolescence and shrinking state budgets. But as of eleven months ago, all that had changed.

He'd met a woman at a New York party and fallen deliriously, sexually, in love. In the process, he'd left a childless marriage filled with frictionless boredom and leaped across the country to be with his new love in a single life-altering jump. Anabella was a forty-year-old woman with two teenage sons who worked as a research scientist in a field—fragrance chemistry—about which Potash was utterly ignorant. He wasn't used to having children in his life; he wasn't used to being in the dark about what his wife did; and he wasn't used to waking each morning alongside someone for whom—differently from his ex-wife, a Realtor—money wasn't the first order of the day. Anabella, who'd grown up in a small town in Minnesota, was lean, spiritually athirst, energetic and unassumingly pretty. Plus, she loved sex. After an amicable divorce from his wife, they married immediately. To the marriage Potash brought a sizable nest egg, some of it his elderly parents', entrusted to him for investment purposes, and some of it his own.

"Can I send you some literature in the mail?" he remembered Janelle Styles asking him after she'd finished her pitch.

"Of course," he'd said, and hesitated a moment before obligingly giving her his mailing address. An envelope was couriered over the very next day, and he made a point of studying the prospectuses, investment strategy and projected return schedules carefully. Years immersed in school budget battles had given him an eye for reading contracts, and he knew his way around a spreadsheet. On the surface anyway, it all checked out perfectly.

Several days later, following up, she called. Cautious by nature, but drawn to the possibility of blessing his new marriage with a whopping annuity while he spent several months shopping around for a new job, Potash agreed to meet for lunch. He arrived on time at the restaurant and paused a moment on the threshold of the entrance. A pretty woman of about thirty, dressed in a black pencil skirt, high heels and a fitted top, stood up from a nearby booth and gave him a brilliant smile.

Potash smiled back, involuntarily, and in response, her own smile deepened on the spot. In some very subtle way, she gave the impression that she'd already calculated for the small, ongoing shock wave that her presence caused among men. Was this simple sophistication, or something else? Her hand was extended toward his in greeting, and her wide, extravagantly lashed green eyes fixed on his and then blinked in a quick triplet.

"Hi, John," she said.

"Janelle, a pleasure." He grasped her hand in his while her other hand fashioned a kind of loose, weaving gesture in the air and came to rest against his shoulder. It lay there for a second while they spoke, light but persistent. He noticed it.

The maître d' took them as if by design to a booth in a darker, quieter part of the restaurant, well away from other diners.

"Have you been here before?" she asked as they sat down.

"Never, actually."

"Oh, good. I find it's the perfect place to meet someone, because it gives that sense of being just a little bit out of the world, and thereby a little bit intimate, unto itself."

"Nice."

She gave him a heatless smile, and he now understood where that plush telephone vibrato of hers came from: her entire body, somehow, was a sounding board for her voice.

"Drink?" she asked.

"No, thanks," he said, "although maybe . . ."

"I know, at lunch, right?" She laughed, familiarly, with square, even teeth bleached almost too white but not quite. "But a spritzer tends to go down easy and still leaves you refreshed."

"Touché," he said gallantly. "A spritzer then!"

When the man left, nearly simultaneously, they both opened their menus.

"So," she said, "how long have you been living in sunshine central?"

"About ten months."

"A newbie! Would it be too forward of me to ask what brought you out here?"

"Well, not to put too fine a point on it, I fell in love."

"Really?" She looked up at him, openmouthed. "Does that still happen? Oh, God," she touched her breast, "I'm sorry if I sound cynical!"

"Not at all," said Potash, smiling. "But what can I say? I'm very happy. And I find that Northern California agrees with me. For a former New Yorker, it's kind of like Disneyland."

"You answered my next question, but I had a feeling."

"What about?"

"That you were from the Northeast."

"Why? Do I give off a big-city vibe?"

"Yes, but I mean that only in the best noncynical way."

She laughed again, in a way that suggested an expansion of some kind, a reminder of the warm-blooded physicality behind her clothes. Potash leaned forward confidentially. "To tell you the truth, I'm still adjusting to being cheerful all the time. It's a new sensation."

"Bottle and sell it, if you can."

The waiter passed again with their drinks and took their orders. She raised her glass, looked at him sportively over its edges, and winked.

"To a successful partnership and a greener earth."

"Amen to that."

They clinked glasses and drank.

And what happened next, thought Potash, finishing his long shower at last and stepping out into the chill, dry air before vigorously wiping himself down with a fresh towel, was what he would have to live with for the rest of his life. Because after three rounds of spritzers, and a stream of dazzling conversation about algae fuel, biomass and ethanol, he agreed to meet her and her "partners" at the nearby home offices of their firm, to discuss the possibility of "bringing him more seriously on board."

Potash finished toweling off and then dressed, slipped on his Merrells and tiptoed out of the bedroom. The tape in his head had stopped playing for him long enough to again appreciate the nest of creaturely amenities in which he found himself. Love had brought him to this home, whose continued existence—as he walked down the main staircase and into the sun-flooded living room through air faintly scented with bougainvillea and piñon pine—depended on his now doing the exact right thing. He went into the kitchen, opened the heavy vault of the fridge door, and drank a glass of orange juice, fast, standing up. Then he strolled out the front door and swung into his SUV. His appointment with Agent Hiram Bortz of the FBI was in two hours and the office was nearly a hundred miles away. Traffic would be ramping up soon and he was hoping, for once, to beat the morning rush.

CHAPTER FOUR

The doctor stood before her, as tall as a tower, dressed all in white and leaning close. Bending forward, he scraped his nails along the soles of her feet.

"Tell me," he said, "do you often lose your balance and fall down a ballroom length of marble stairs?"

There was a silence.

"And do you have any idea how lucky you are?"

She didn't know how lucky she was. She was in the hospital. What could that possibly have to do with luck? She wanted to speak, but the words wouldn't come. The words were still hanging a distance off. The doctor was looking at her with his peculiar smile-frown.

"In addition to everything else," he said, "the blunt force trauma to the skull produced a subdural hematoma that came very, very close to shutting you down. I wouldn't say you're a miracle, young lady, but you're one whole heck of a medical outlier."

The doctor then leaned close enough so that she could feel the soft, buttery lapping of his breath.

"Lucky life," he whispered.

She shut her eyes, and when she next opened them a man in a blue suit was standing there smiling. His hair had a wet, seal-like glisten to it, and a box of beautiful air seemed to stand out around the bones of his face.

"You're up," he said in a soft small voice entirely unlike the big man he was. "Mind if I sit?"

"No," she said carefully.

With a hissing sound, he sat on a chair by her bed. She tried not to stare too hard at this person, who was telling her he was a police detective named Dan France and giving her a card embossed with a tiny gold shield while smiling at her with his face of an intelligent, well-fed animal. Soon after, he was leaning forward and touching the tips of his fingers together between his legs and drawing a breath. Clearly he was about to tell her something important. But all she heard as he began to speak was how his voice had the exact pitch of the outboard motor on a boat her family had once owned called Nutmeg, *which thrummed as it somehow said the human words:* slidepath, likelihood, propulsive, motive.

After that, time passed or maybe it just stood still while her mind contracted into a shape that snapped like a whip as it shot her all the way around space and suddenly back into herself, dazed, looking up into the man's handsome face.

"You fell asleep for a second," Mr. Dan France said.

"Oh."

"It's common with your condition."

"Is it?"

"I was talking about what you could remember of the seconds that preceded your, uh, fall."

"Okay."

"I'm looking forward to talking to you again, Margot."

She wanted to say the right thing, but now too many words came forward, confusing her; they hung sparkling in the space before the eyes of her mind while making a tiny clattering sound, like the applause of dimes, before shooting away in every direction. She followed them as far as she could before she fell asleep.

When she next opened her eyes—a day later? A week?—Dan France was again, incredibly, standing at the foot of her bed. He was blinking lashes as long as a cartoon animal and slowly opening and closing his mouth.

But before Dan France there had been the mirror. She remembered that now. She remembered that a helpful nurse had held it up to her. In the mirror her face was a broken, perfectly round object, like a dropped clock.

"Good morning," he was saying.

"Good morning?"

"I was in the area and thought I'd stop in," he said.

"You ...."

"How you feeling?"

Her voice when she now spoke buzzed softly in the cavity of her head.

"I'm not sure."

"Tired, sad, happy, any of those ring a bell?"

There was a very long pause while she flung the lariat of her mind at some floating words, yanked them in.

"A joke?"

He laughed out loud. It was pleasant laughter, friendly laughter. It meant no harm. Maybe he was one of those boring harmless handsome men.

"Mind if I sit down for a moment?"

The lariat expanded into space, snickered back:

"Suit yourself."

She shrugged her shoulders to accompany what she'd said. But that was a mistake; a stabbing pain shot through her arm.

"Whoa," he said. "Take it easy."

Words were coming back to her, and with them a certain familiar pressure, light, sour, warm: words.

"One day at a time," he said.

"Right," she said, because it was what you said, and because he was continuing to smile, was the pretty animal-like Dan France, and because she liked the feeling of receiving that smile across the air of the room, like something tossed lightly and lovingly.

"You're funny," he said.

"I am?"

"Yes, you make all these expressions, like you're thinking terribly and deeply about everything you say, and then maybe a single word pops out. Oh, wait, I'm sorry, I didn't mean that!"

She was crying. There had been no intervening moment; the water had simply appeared in her eyes and begun falling down her face. She'd been thinking about the mirror again. He jumped to his feet and raised his arms in the air like someone surrendering at gunpoint.

"Not what I wanted!" He dropped his arms. "Here, please. I'm so sorry."

His handkerchief was out and coming toward her. Cloudlike, it was scented with something that was maybe lavender.

"Anything you need," Dan France was saying with his police voice as she buried her face in the scented cloud. "Anything I can do, you just let me know, okay?"

She was nodding. He was seating himself again at the foot of her bed. He was opening his mouth and she was looking into that mouth. It occurred to her how nice it'd be to go to sleep in that mouth, with her feet hanging out.

That special old warm feeling was coming back to her; that feeling of being in a body again. Below the broken face were her arms and legs. Without warning she dropped off to sleep and began falling slowly through a deep, dimensional mist a little bit like the seaside fogs of childhood into which she remembered inserting whole parts of herself disappearingly: toes, knees, thighs vanishing as if into milk.

When she dropped out of that cloud, landing gently on her feet and looking around, she was twelve years old. She was in a store that extended in every direction as far as the eye could see. Gingerly she moved forward down aisles that seemed piled high as if with all the goods of the world. She raised an arm and looked carefully, once, around the store. Her hair was perfectly combed and brushed. Her pinafore was fresh from the dryer. Her Buster Browns were polished to a T. She smiled politely. And then she stole something.

Lying in her hospital bed, her eyes swimming in smooth figure eights beneath her lids, she smiled.

She'd begun by stealing small stuff mainly: costume jewelry; cassette tapes. The desire to do so was like a small, kindly tug on the sleeve. It pulled her to the nearby malls, where she would walk in her quiet observant way through the lighted barns of the stores. She'd nod calmly at the passersby. She'd enter the stores. And she'd steal from them.

At home she spent her spare time reading of women trapped in remote country settings and dying for love. She read Northanger Abbey. *She read* Jane Eyre. *She wrote in her diary in a flowing hand using a fountain pen that she felt somehow linked her up to the history of suffering women in the nineteenth century. From the local Safeway she filched tea bags, croissants, and puff pastries. At the Stop and Shop she lifted small bottles of perfume.*

Evenings, she watched her father's face carefully at the dinner table to see if he knew. He knew everything. His head was a repository of all the knowledge in the world. And she loved to watch his mouth as he spoke. The power came from there. As did the lack of doubt in everything he said. This was an amazing thing. How could you live without doubt? Life was so filled with it.

But from her father instead there came this absolute sureness and unswerving speed. Everything he did was fast. He ate his food fast and with swift square motions. In his car, down Route 6, he moved quickly. And once the car came to a stop with a quick screech and the door whipped open, then out he came, charging into the very next thing and tilted forward with velocity. In his study, in the living room of the house, her father moved with his loping stride. He steered his tall frame past the room where she crouched practicing her violin. He was en route to the bottle of whiskey in his study. Meanwhile the tempo of her Czerny exercises increased. Harsh squawks and rubbing whistles awoke from the instrument. It occurred to her, lying asleep in her hospital bed, that as a child she called to her father with her instrument as a bird calls to another, and that the finger exercises on her violin that she remembered unhappily filling the house with their cawing music were in fact the passionate cries of her loneliness.

She was lonely, in the little house on the edge of the earth. The continent finished there, in that plunge into the bean-green water near Cape Cod. You could stand on that small chilly bit of sand feeling the grains between your toes and you could stare to where the earth curved, and launch your gaze into outer space.

She opened her eyes in her hospital bed. Dan France was long gone and the room was dark. Things hissed and twittered in the night, and in the hallway outside her door, every few minutes she heard the faint sucking sound of the ripple-soled shoes of the nurses. She lay there for a long time, unmoving. If she shut her eyes, she knew, it would start all over again.

CHAPTER FIVE

As promised, Margot booked a private lesson through his website, and on the morning of that lesson, Lawrence found himself in an unnaturally good mood. Having had breakfast with his wife, Glynis, he returned to his study to attend to some paperwork and was ready to leave the house by 10:30 A.M.

"All dolled up today?" Glynis said to him as he passed her in the kitchen, where she was misting the orchids with a long-necked brass spray can. He was nattily attired in lightweight summer slacks, a white dress shirt and loafers. She was wearing Crocs, cargo shorts and a shapeless linen top. Having just recently finished gardening, she had her sun hat drawn low on her head.

"I've got a private."

"Really? You look like you've got a screen test."

Small, clean puffs of mist came between his glance and her face at that moment, and on either side of them, they laughed.

Darling, he thought to himself. But he did not say it. Instead, continuing to walk away, Lawrence shot a furtive look at his wife as she stood in a pose as familiar to him as the smell of his own body: watchful, with down-lowered eyes and the strong planes of the cheekbones catching the light. Over the many years of their marriage, he had found a peace in discarding his own perceptions of her aging and then, when he could no longer ignore them, embracing them as proofs testifying to the unshakable eternity of their bond: *we're going out of this life together.* At fifty-three, despite the Jazzercise classes and the daily time spent bowing and twisting with the Wii in front of the television, she was beginning to expand everywhere at once, like a reverse invasion. Yet on certain days, at certain moments, the right play of light and shadow could still counterfeit a perfect image of the fresh, apple-shaped face he'd first fallen in love with. These instants of silent time travel he found intensely moving. It was unfair that men as they grew older drew into a configuration called "dignified," while women, despite the pots and paints of their cosmetics, stood nakedly exposed to the depredations of age. Small brown spots high on her temples had recently appeared, as if Death, daubing with a brush, was getting in its first licks.

"I'm off," he said, hefting his shoulder bag.

She raised her eyes to him and sent a few more tentative puffs of vapor into the long-stemmed, swaying clump of flowers.

"Good-bye, honey," she said.

He raised his hand to blow her a kiss, unconsciously brushing with the pads of his fingers the colorless stitch of a scar. It was the signature of that moment, at the age of twenty-five, when Lawrence had been in a bar and gotten into a fight. Back then he'd had a bit of a hair-trigger temper, and the years spent in high school and then college lacrosse had endowed him with physical strength allied to an innate aggressivity. A couple of strong drinks in him and he'd be halfway spoiling for a showdown. On this particular night, some stray drunken comment by a passerby about the girl he was with ignited him; a shouted exchange led to him receiving a slap, and not long after, Lawrence was swinging his fists in wide, swift arcs from his hips.

He'd fought before, without incident. But this time, after the man sucker-punched him so hard in the face as to have perforated his upper lip with a tooth, he swung back blindly, on instinct, connecting satisfyingly with the man's jaw and sending him reeling backward. The man tripped and slammed the back of his head full force against the fieldstone edge of the bar before hitting the floor and losing consciousness. When not long after he went into a long series of open-eyed violent convulsions, it was clear he'd had more than the wind knocked out of him.

The young man, a promising grad student in a local business school, had sustained damage to the occipital lobe of the brain and would thereafter suffer permanently from visual field cuts and movement agnosia. Lawrence became very familiar with these terms because they were employed with punitive precision at the civil trial by lawyers hired by the boy's family. Wheelchair bound, speaking softly, the boy made a terrific witness. Lawrence avoided jail time and bankruptcy only because friends of his who had been there that night came forward at the trial to bolster his claim of self-defense.

But alone, in that period, he grew sick with remorse. He was unable to reconcile this magnesium-flash of violence with his self-image as someone versed in the arts of reconciliation and gifted with a second sight into the occult essence of the world. Long after he'd abandoned the volatility of his twenties, the bar fight continued to live on inside him as a pressurized cell of memory, warping the flow of experience around it in such a way as to sway him from a long-considered career in law enforcement and drawing him eventually into the windless harbor of a field—psychology—where the violence was only verbal. A brief clinical practice and a short teaching career prepared him for what would be his adult mission: writing bestselling books on the secrets of face and body reading, and conducting what would eventually become large, lucrative seminars on the same subject.

Having kissed his wife good-bye, Lawrence now drove to the motel that housed the small conference room he rented for his occasional privates. A half hour later he was setting up the dry-erase board on its easel, and breaking out his notes, when he heard a disturbance at the door and saw her there. Dressed in tight black pants, a designer white T-shirt and sneakers, she looked somewhat like a mature college student, even though he'd guess her age somewhere in her late twenties.

"Well, hi!" she said loudly.

"Margot, welcome."

Holding out his large hand, he shook her dainty fingers while feeling himself internally contracting at the same time. She made him naturally watchful.

"Please sit down," he said, with a little bow.

"Thank you."

She slid her laptop onto the table, took out a notebook, and, as well, he was gratified to see, a copy of *The Physique of Finance*.

"I've now read you twice," she said, smiling, "with a pencil!"

"Always nice to hear." He laced his hands together and smiled. He was seated about four feet away from her.

"Have a pleasant drive here?" he asked.

"Not bad, considering the traffic at this time of the day can stop you in your tracks," she said.

"Don't I know it."

Unbeknownst to her, he was studying her intensely. The small bumps and thinness of her shell-like ears; the precise curl and fold of her lip; the way in which the hair of the brows was distributed in two circumflex hoops above her bright green eyes—he felt his own eyes drop infinitesimally and then flutter, tabulating his perceptions, storing them away.

"Well," he said, nodding, "shall we begin?"

"Please," she said, nodding, as she opened her laptop and set her notebook out in front of her. Though her hand had felt fragile in his, he noted that she actually had fine, strong hands, indicating a person gifted in doing and achieving in the world. Her nails were ridgeless and attested to a diet rich in vitamin B and iron, but the moons, he noticed, were invisible: pituitary problems?

"Any thought where you'd like to begin?" he asked. "What needs strengthening and work?"

"Thanks for asking," she said. "I think that what I need most to work on is how best to make a good first impression. I mean, once the ice is broken, I'm usually pretty good, but sometimes I just freeze up while still on the approach ramp. Does this make sense?"

"Absolutely." He'd been nodding as he listened, and then he stopped. "The Golden Gate," he said simply.

"Pardon?"

"The Golden Gate." He stood up and wrote the words on the dry-erase board, and then turned to her. "It's the key ten-second interval when you meet someone for the first time and they form their lasting first impression of you. That gate is crossed by trust, blocked by fear, and negotiated, as is often the case," he looked over the tops of his glasses at her—"by desire."

She was staring back at him, slightly openmouthed, while her hands, as if seemingly independent organisms, produced a high, fast cricketing from the keyboard.

"Cool," she said.

"To unlock that gate," he said, "we each of us lead with our attributes. Some are visual, some are emotional and intellectual, and some, if we believe our brothers on the esoteric side of the aisle, are subtler than that."

"Subtler?" Her fingers were poised motionless over the keys.

"Let me ask you a few questions," he said. "Did you know that retailers sell more in blue environments than in red ones?"

Her fingers jerked into motion again.

"Or that shoppers consistently purchase more expensive merchandise when classical music is played in the background?"

He could see her face relaxing. "Did you know that haircuts, for at least a week, have a direct effect on endorphin production?"

"No," she said, "I didn't."

"Or that the voices of people with what is called 'greater bilateral body symmetry,' which is fancy talk for a good body, are rated as sounding more attractive than those with less symmetrical bodies? Their voices, mind you—"

"I think I see where you might be—"

"Going with this?" He smiled. "My point," he said, "is that things aren't necessarily what they appear at first, especially in our line of work. We deal with the liminal, Margot, with the partial, the hidden. To the experienced reader, faces and bodies are like a kabbalistic text in which every word stands for something other than what it seems."

"Kabbalistic? I like the way you think," she said.

"Excellent," he said, and beamed. He was feeling sharp and he was feeling expansive. He turned a forty-five-degree angle, splayed his hand at the juncture of his lumbar and midback regions, and rotated farther, sending out a fusillade of dry cracks.

"I have a little handout," he said, centering himself, "just for you."

But she didn't respond to that. She was still studying him a second. "It looks like you could use an adjustment on your back," she said, and seemed about to say something else. But before she could, Lawrence cut in smoothly, "Couldn't we all."

Out of a loose-leaf notebook he took a small paper-clipped bundle of papers with the handwritten title: *First Impact*.

"Now let's dig in," he said.

CHAPTER SIX

Potash almost beat rush hour, en route to the FBI offices. But as he drew near to San Francisco, the traffic thickened, and then slowed to a crawl, and the anxiety this brought on naturally tipped him into retrospective mode. From there, it was but a quick, associative leap to regret. His regret at the moment was vast, foundational. Where to begin? He could start with the fact that, after his lunch meeting with Janelle Styles, he was in a very good mood, expansive, sanguine, and more in love with the new woman of his life than ever.

More mundanely, he remembered (while sitting in the crawling car and glancing occasionally out the side window to where people frolicked in the surf and early morning sun worshippers, already on the beach, lay foreshortened like inkblots on the sand) that he phoned some friends back in New York and asked them to dig into the specific sustainable investment areas Greenleaf Financial was proposing. The word that came back was that several of these areas were, in fact, on the techno-cultural cusp and currently attracting a lot of heat among sustainably oriented forward-thinking investors. Greenleaf's deal flow might not be quite on par with blue-chip venture capital firms like Kleiner Perkins or Benchmark, but it was close. Bolstered by the flood of positive information, he was encouraged to set up a meeting with the Greenleaf staff.

Would he ever forget Janelle's face that day? Would he ever not remember exactly how she looked as she came out of an inner door to the waiting room with her arms open wide and her head lying slightly to one side while crying, "John, so excited to see you!" Now slumped in the stopped car and muttering to himself, Potash turned on the radio to the calming New Age "space music" station he and Anabella so loved, which was heavy on ouds and lutes. As he did so, he remembered her pulling him into a frontal full-contact hug that went on so long a strange, mixed heat blossomed upward from his thorax. When the hug stopped, Janelle, looking carefully into his eyes, drew her mouth into a smile.

"Well, how simply great to see you again," she said.

"Yes," he said, feeling the sudden need to scratch his forehead energetically, "you too."

"And welcome to Greenleaf," she went on.

"Glad to be here."

She did a quarter turn with her arms in the air like a ballerina, drawing his attention irresistibly to how her body funneled downward from her breasts to her waist, and asked, "Would you like a coffee?"

"At this time of day? I'd—I'd be dancing all night."

"Ha, right you are! Well, then," she turned back to face him directly. "To business, yes?"

"Absolutely."

"Right this way. Frank and Nick are already here."

He was then escorted down a small windowless hallway, headed toward a conference room. A man stood up from a conference table as he entered the room and bid him a crisp "Hello, sir!" This was Frank Mayfair. Shaggily gray-haired and bearded and somewhere in his midfifties, Frank wore a blue double-breasted blazer with double rows of brass sleeve buttons and was clearly, self-consciously of the school of "salty old dog."

"Glad you could make it to our port of call," he said with astonishing adherence to type, putting out his hand to shake with a small tinkle of bracelets. Was that an odd musk Potash was smelling, or aftershave covering up the metabolized funk of alcohol? Meanwhile, behind him, Nick Lattanzio was standing up. Unsmiling and small, Nick had dark hair combed straight back and seemed possessed by a variety of subtle nervous tremors.

"Hi," Nick said simply, extending a slightly damp palm.

"As you know," Janelle interrupted before he could get much of a bead on Nick, "we have much to get to today, so let's begin, shall we?" Once they were seated, she leaned forward and cleared her throat. "I'm very excited to bring John on board. Not only does he have a genuine desire to be involved in sustainable venture investment, he also happens to be a good guy. And by the way," she stage-whispered, "he's a New Yorker in exile."

Potash allowed himself a smile.

"Frank," she said, "why don't you begin our presentation."

"Aye-aye," said Frank, shooting him a wink and clearing his throat.

After a moment, seeming to think better of it, he got to his feet, and Potash was surprised to see, below the immaculate blue blazer, a pair of somewhat ratty jeans.

"In our world of modern conveniences," he began, "it's easy to forget the one deep truth about life, which is that we live within nature's boundaries. John, natural resources are the assets on our planetary balance sheet, and oil and natural gas, to take two examples out of about ten thousand, are being drawn down daily. Imagine," Frank beetled his brows as if in indignation "a company that systematically depleted its own assets without any plan to replenish them. Can you imagine the hell *those* people would catch at the shareholders' meeting? Well, those people are us, John, and the shareholders' meeting is the national election, and guess what? Nothing changes, no matter who's in office. But we at Greenleaf Financial believe different. We believe in plain talking and bottom lines. For us, profit isn't necessarily the enemy of sane environmental policy. It's an enabler!"

Potash nodded grudgingly. He wasn't about to be bowled over by simple volume, or the usual arpeggios of sustainability and planetary threat. And Frank, nearly as if he understood that, immediately switched gears, and began talking with technical precision about the exact composition of the fund of which Potash would be a part. As he spoke, Nick, like a chorus, would interrupt regularly to speak in a slightly monotone voice about returns and accelerated depreciation schedules. In this way, with one of the pitchers happy and expansive, and the other dourly literal, they moved forward for nearly an hour. When it was over, the meeting was sealed with a valedictory round of happy handshakes, after which Janelle walked Potash out to his car. She seemed to bounce slightly as she strode. Potash, who was carrying under his arm a laminated plastic folder blazoned with the vaguely planetary logo of the company and stuffed with letterhead bearing a variety of financial breakdowns, felt his head buzzing from the hour-long pitch and his own proximity to all that luscious, ecologically sound, socially boastable revenue.

"Wow," Janelle said, touching him on the forearm as they walked, her green eyes sparkling. "I mean, John." She laughed. "You're good!"

"Am I?"

She held her finger on his forearm, her voice firm: "Yes, you are. You ask questions, you make inquiries, you're really engaged, and you know what you're talking about. Impressive, my friend."

"Well, thank you," said Potash, who enjoyed the compliment, even as he gave his own performance a B, nothing more. Yes, he had requested breakdowns of some of the projected claims, and yes, he knew that among the financial instruments the fund would be involved in was something called a reverse shell merger, which was how a promising young business, by attaching itself to a publicly traded but essentially dead company, could float a stock offering without having to deal with Sarbanes-Oxley and all the legal and accounting expense of a traditional IPO. But there was also a whole blizzard of terms that were beyond him—though he'd dutifully filled up his yellow pad with notes.

"There's a lot to digest. But rest assured," he said, beaming at her, "digest it I will."

"Of course you will." Her beautiful head, exactly three feet from his, swam along next to him with the unwavering horizontal smoothness of a Steadicam. "Remember, John, that for us, every client relationship is a partnership. And we personally invest in every one of our offerings, which allows us to align our interests perfectly with yours. I was pleased with the results from the Dynaventure Fund, which I chalk up as a solid double. But this time, my friend, we're going for a home run."

They passed through the swinging glass doors and into the parking lot. "I'm impressed," Potash admitted. "And that Frank," he said, "is some character."

She stopped a moment on the asphalt and put her hand on her breast, forcing Potash to convert his next forward step to a kind of pirouette as he swiveled back around to face her.

"Francis Mayfair is one of the best, the cleanest, and by the way the most profitable Wall Street brains in the business."

"Is he? Funny that I never—"

"He belongs," she went on, holding his eye, "to the generation of the Milkens and Buffetts and Kravises and has their same brainpower. But rather than mindlessly pursuing money for just money's sake, he's found that ethics and mission are entirely compatible with outsize profits. The man shines a light, even if he likes staying under the radar. But you should see his spread in Costa Rica!"

"Does he sail his own boat there?"

She laughed. "You mean the beard? He does seem a bit 'nautical' and yachty, doesn't he. You're funny."

They began walking again and soon drew up to his car.

"To get serious a second, John," she said, "the ball's now in your court. Go home, talk to your friends, your brokers, complete your due diligence and then get back to us when you've come to a point of resolution. As we made clear, we're not looking for a hands-off, passive investor who remembers us only when we wire his quarterlies into his account. We prefer actively engaged strategic partners that we can leverage for domain knowledge. And as a perk for privileged fund participants, by the way"—she leaned forward confidentially—"you'll have access to our London office, which is, well, *lovely.*"

She put a special, curling emphasis on the last word.

"Swinging Londontown, eh?" He felt suddenly giddy as he opened the car door, and in a single smooth motion lowered the window while taking his seat. "I'm there!"

"Good," she leaned forward into the open window while bringing the cleft between her exposed breasts, like the notched sight of a rifle, directly into his line of vision. "Bye-bye, John."

"Bye for now, Janelle."

She turned and sauntered back to the building and, grinning to himself, Potash put the key in the ignition, bursting with his secret: that he was about to make him and his wife pots and pots of money, and thereby add yet another link to the golden chain of circumstance that had begun assembling itself from the moment he'd left New York to start a beautiful, sustainable, humanly rich new life in California.

A horn blared behind him and he raised his eyes from his sad daydream to see—finally!—a lane of space opening ahead of him. Traffic, ever mysterious, had unknotted for reasons known only to itself, and he accelerated toward the FBI office. After making good progress for about twenty minutes, he turned off the interstate and was soon following the curving road along the route he'd MapQuested. He parked, hustled out of the SUV and took the stairs two at a time. Finding the proper door, he entered and gave his name to the receptionist. The room was furnished in the typical pastel governmental palette of advanced desertification, and some worn magazines were piled on a table. Potash picked one up, and unseeing, began paging through it. They were superbusy that morning, the receptionist had explained, and he'd have to wait.

CHAPTER SEVEN

The days had a swimming, circular rhythm to them. The sun came up. The nurses bustled around the room. An open calm space expanded around her, and she lay partly in that space and partly in the silence she felt inside herself. Then the sun burned out and evening came on, crawling up the sides of the room like ink filling a jar, and the process was repeated.

The doctor smelled of peppermint. He shined a light in her eyes and spoke in a prying, anxious voice about her progress. Nicer by far was Dan France, who came by regularly, and who often, as now, was waiting on her, smiling pleasantly as if a second had gone by, when she opened her eyes.

"And so?" he said.

"And so?" she repeated, slowly.

"You were in the middle of telling me everything," he said, and then looked at her as if he knew something, and gave her a long, liquid wink.

Irresistibly, her eyes slid lower. When they closed, she again found herself looking directly into the bright, fresh faces of the eighth-grade boys in her middle-school class. They bulged and dwindled hilariously in their bodies, and if she let them kiss her, they made gulping sounds like toilets. But one grade higher was a teacher named Mr. Wilkington, who gazed at her with a strange calm doglike intent that made her feel he was trying to touch her heart through her clothes. She liked that. He had a beard like a wild animal and was terribly thin. He had wanted to be a poet once, he told her in an afterschool conference, and when she told him that she loved poetry, particularly the Lake Poets, and that she loved many things to do with certain parts of England in the nineteenth century, he was so surprised that for a full long moment the normally chatty Mr. Wilkington couldn't speak.

Not long after, a book appeared in her library cubbyhole. It was a collection of poetry by a man named Thomas Hardy. It was very beautiful and very sad. Thomas Hardy's wife had died and he missed her terribly.

> Can it be you that I hear? Let me view you, then,
> Standing as when I drew near to the town
> Where you would wait for me: yes, as I knew you then,
> Even to the original air-blue gown!

In her diary she wrote, "I've met the most unusual man. He's funny and cool and he always looks to one side in conversation with you like he's hoping an invisible person sitting next to him will know the exact right thing to say and he can then say that thing. I think I'm going to seduce him."

They began meeting after school. They would sometimes take walks along the nearby drainage canal. He was directing her along the list of his favorite books and they would discuss her reading. She'd never heard anyone talk like him. For her father, words were a series of cold, functional links in a chain, but Mr. Wilkington with his voice like a sad woodwind spoke in looping long expeditions of thought. Ideas moved him. He was terribly excited. Then he was misty-eyed with longing. Then he was battered by insights that he nearly choked on trying to explain. The letters of John Keats to Fanny Brawne were "what doom tasted like on the tongue." Shelley had "a heart like autumn." Poetry "should be taken in small doses every day, like vitamins."

Then one day the gentle Mr. Wilkington sat her down on a bench and said, "I love your company, Margot. In fact I love it so much that I realize that I can't do this with you any longer. It's not right that a teacher take walks with a girl student, especially one of whom he's as terribly fond as I am of you. I'm sorry, but we're going to have to break this off, sparrow. Okay?"

That night, with tears rolling down her cheeks, she wrote, "This is what it feels like to be heartbroken. It's like being stuffed with ice except the ice burns. It's like being the last person alive on the planet and only seeing dead people everywhere you look. I solemnly swear I'll never ever let it happen again as long as I live!"

Later that same year, her mother came down with a disease whose ugly name sounded in her head like leg braces and rattling metal. This was multiple sclerosis. And though the reasons for the illness were "unknown," her mother withdrew to her bed and began spending most of each day prone while wearing a faint funny smile on her new face like she alone knew what was the matter and wasn't telling.

Her father began arriving home from work with red blotches on his cheeks and then steering his long body unsteadily to his study, where he fell asleep in his sea-green Barcalounger chair and slept right through dinner and sometimes the next breakfast too. His voice turned slack. More than once he parked the car at a diagonal on the front lawn. Sloppy stains appeared on his clothes from meals falling from *his hands. The town was small. Children in school made ugly faces at her. They pointed at her the stinking finger of accusation, the finger of ridicule:*

Your father is a drunk!

My father is an important lawyer who works for the attorney general of Massachusetts said the cold, calm voice in her head. But she never said it aloud; she never defended him. She continued implacably to get straight As at school. She practiced the violin every night for hours. She watched her mother exhausting herself by flinging herself like a wave against the large rocklike silence of her father, and it didn't matter. "I will be married," she wrote in her diary. "I have to be married. Nothing can stop me from being married," she wrote.

CHAPTER EIGHT

After three classroom lessons, Lawrence convened their fourth meeting in the street. He called it his "live laboratory." He chose a small inclined street he'd used before for drills of this kind, which had an outdoor café at its uppermost point. Arriving first, he seated himself at a table and ordered a coffee.

The plan was for Margot to station herself about a hundred yards down the hill and ask directions of ten passersby while charting as many facial tells as possible during the conversations. While pretending to take down the information being offered her, she would in reality note these facial tells on a small pad. Lawrence would form his own conclusions about the same people as they strolled past his table a couple of minutes later and they would then compare notes.

He had brought the daily paper and was scanning the headlines when he heard her swift stride.

"Good morning," she said, coming up to his table.

He looked up, smiling. Because it was warm out she was wearing shorts, a halter top and platform espadrilles. Her brunette hair was pulled back in a chignon and her makeup was skewed to a summer palette. It had not escaped his notice that she was an expert in the shape-shifting use of cosmetics and clothes. When they first met, she'd had the wholesome balanced face of a young soccer mom. Subsequent meetings had revealed her equally at home dressed with an aggressive downtown, even punkish edge. Today she was fully inhabiting the role of artsy coed. And the striking green eyes were as mascaraed as ever. He told himself that the warm burst of feeling he was entertaining just then was simply the hunger of a childless father for a daughter in life.

"Morning, Margot," he said, "and don't you look perfect for the job today."

"I thought I'd work my blend-in look," she said. "And you look well."

Lawrence had a large, calm, open face of the kind that people regularly referred to as "wholesome," with square teeth, wide brown eyes, a domed forehead and the gray quills of hair usually brushed straight back while still wet. His mouth, however, was small and firm.

"Thank you, and your blend-in look is working," he said. "You're so good you're almost invisible."

She frowned a second.

"Just kidding," he said quickly, and then, confused at the sudden, open hanging feeling in the air, he went on with a quickening professional tone, "Um, I usually send students to that spot down there."

She turned and squinted into the sun, down the hill, while he found himself studying her lean jawline.

"Remember," he said slowly, "that it's important to distract these people and send their minds elsewhere as a way to get a deeper, better look. And here's a little bit of neurolinguistic programming for background. Most people in the world are right-handed. When right-handers are creating an image in their minds, their eyes generally look up to the right, okay?"

"Sure," she said, a little noncommittally.

"But if they're recalling something they've heard, like an old song, they look to the left and tilt their head as if listening. If they are remembering a feeling, like say a physical sensation or an emotion, they look down and to the right. People talking silently to themselves also look down to the left. It's like a compass rose of a sort. And why is this important?"

She'd begun smiling, as she always did when she received new information. "I'm sure you're gonna tell me," she said.

"It's important because if we know whether someone typically thinks in pictures, or words or feelings, then we're that much closer to their decision points, and that much better at making predictive guesses about their next move. The smallest advantage is better than none at all."

"I love it," she said. She was making her tiny upper body swerves again.

"Good," he replied. The warm feeling in his chest was deepening. "I'm giving you thirty minutes, Margot. You bring the steno pad?"

She pulled it from her pocket.

"Check," she said.

"Well, then, go for it."

"Wish me luck."

"As my Italian grandfather used to say, '*In boca al lupo*.'"

"Which means?" She was already half turned around and facing down the hill.

"In the mouth of the wolf."

Lightly, nearly over her shoulder, she flung the words, "And would the wolf be you?" After which, she sauntered down the hill.

Lawrence raised his paper halfway up as a screen, and over it he watched her take up her position. Within minutes, an old man wandered by and she convinced him to stop for what seemed like an extended time. A minute later she was nodding gravely to a librarian-looking lady of late middle age and then a teenage boy. He watched how she carefully arranged her body in such a way as to invite or remain neutral, depending on the situation. She did this by sucking in her breasts or throwing them into relief and by tilting her hips in such a way as to either "shine" or "cover" her pelvis while moving her hands distractingly. Two male college students stopped to talk and he laughed with silent appreciation as he watched her draw them toward her so that by the end of the conversation they were both raked forward on their toes.

Lawrence ordered a second coffee and by the time it arrived, these same people were approaching his table and his eager eyes. Would they have the indented temples of the obsessive-compulsive? The cleft chin of the attention seeker? Would they sport the short eyebrows of the friendless or the downturned nose of the shrewd? Differently from the fallen world of speech, the body never lied. Were they sporting the high blink rate of liars? Or, if they were a couple, was one of them practicing "ventral denial"—that is, rotating the sensitive front part of their body significantly away from their partner?

Together, they worked the passersby on the street for about a half hour. It was a sunny warm morning, and the coffee tasted good in his mouth, and the peacefulness of the situation, along with his own pleasure in exercising his craft, relaxed and soothed him. But before he could comment on it to himself, she strode swiftly back up the hill and beat him to the punch.

"Can I tell you something?" she said as she sat down next to him and he felt that energetic wave of hers wash over him.

"Yes," he said.

"I felt fantastic out there."

"I could tell."

"No, I mean it was like this work, the way it looks inside people, it just gives you this incredible confidence that you can just do whatever you want with someone." She shrugged, as if she were giving too much away. "I guess," she said in a deliberately calmer voice, "I always wanted a little extra protection in life."

"Nothing wrong with that." He was feeling indulgent. "So," he said, "let's see what you got?"

"Okay," she said, and gave him her pad. He was impressed by the congruence between their outlooks. With allowances made for her relative greenness and lack of vocabulary, her intuitive reading of people's appetites and inclinations was nearly spot-on.

"Impressive," he said, smiling.

"Now," she said, lowering her eyes, "you're embarrassing me."

"No, I'm serious." He suddenly wanted her to understand just how good she was; it was important to him. "I've been at this a long time and you're not typical. In fact, you're not not typical by a long shot, which is a funny-sounding thing to say, but you get the idea."

"Consider it gotten, and thank you. I think I always wanted a teacher who I felt was on my level, and I think it's happened to me maybe once before in my life." She paused, looking into his eyes. "Don't take this in the wrong way, but can I do something for you?"

"You already are," he said gallantly. "It makes all the difference in the world to be 'gotten' by someone other than a middle-aged woman in a bad pantsuit who's convinced her hubby is, uh, carrying on"—he pronounced the words carefully—"with his secretary."

"Lawrence—" She did one of those microtonality things again, almost imperceptibly lowering her voice.

"Yes?" he asked.

She placed the tips of her fingers together beneath her chin. She was "steepling." He couldn't believe it! Evidently, she'd forgotten she was making the most superauthoritative and confident tell of them all. Again, he was recalled to the fact that she was a player, possibly a user. He studied her a moment, but without result. What did she want?

"Dinner?" she said. "With me?"

CHAPTER NINE

Potash waited a long, long time for the FBI agent, aimlessly leafing through magazines while rehearsing in his head the particulars of the last few weeks and days. He did this in tribute to his long-standing belief that recollection was a useful response to crisis, and in his conviction that making a story out of it somehow absolved him from the thought he'd been played for an utter moron.

And what *was* the story?

Irritably, he put down the magazine, shutting his eyes. The memory was like a bad smell he couldn't stop smelling. It began in the days after his meeting with Janelle Styles, when he spent many hours on due diligence. The portfolio companies taking part in the offering all had websites that, given the secretive nature of their work, were password protected. Greenleaf had thoughtfully furnished him with these passwords, and he passed several afternoons browsing their "news" sections, which boasted flattering profiles in journals he'd never heard of and reams of jargon-heavy "white papers" published for industry consumption. Having signed a nondisclosure agreement in advance, he savored the sense of elation involved in peering into the inner workings of what he believed, in a very real sense, to be the future. He also cold-called at least two of the experts whose names Greenleaf had provided him and had affable entry-level chats about sustainable energy that quickly spiraled into arcane theoretical regions he couldn't follow.

In all this, Potash was waiting patiently for the arrival of what he privately called his "vector." His vector was his private tipping point, that confluence of hard data, intuition and good vibes that had green-lit all the most important transitional moments of his life. After four days of research and a couple dozen phone calls, the vector arrived suddenly one afternoon. It was accompanied, as was so often the case, by the sense of an abrupt sharpening of vision, of superfine clarity allied to a feeling of specific sanction. *This* was what he was supposed to do, and right this very second. Dimming the lights in his rented office, he turned down the ambient "space music," called his personal banker and instructed him to wire-transfer six hundred and fifty thousand dollars to the Greenleaf EcoTech High Yield Fund.

The resultant euphoria was intense, unnaturally sweet and dramatically short-lived. The very next day, he sat waiting patiently with his wife at a high-end local restaurant to which he'd invited Janelle for a celebratory dinner. His wife, who had never met Janelle and was still in the dark about his investment, had wondered out loud at the expense of the place, but, in a magnanimous mood, he'd ordered drinks for them both followed by a costly bottle of white wine. The EcoTech Fund was going to be a bouquet he laid at Anabella's feet, and extravagance was the order of the evening.

An hour later, he was slightly drunk and growing annoyed. Janelle hadn't arrived, and he couldn't very well phone in front of his wife and upset the elaborately choreographed surprise. Potash took the endless box staircase downstairs to the bathroom, irritated at first. But the irritation soon began to shade into something else as he stood in the low-lit space methodically dialing both Janelle's home and cell numbers and finding them ringing through to voice mail. He tried the numbers of another Greenleaf contact and had the same thing happen. Openly alarmed, he dug through his wallet to find yet another. He dialed those two numbers as well, and then two others. As each of them rang through to the exact same recorded message, he found himself effortlessly ascending a rising arc of panic. Three minutes after having entered the bathroom, Potash put the phone back in his pocket and stared at his face in the mirror. Without warning, a white flare of light went off in his head while a ring of cold sweat burst onto the crown of his skull and he bent double over the sink as a vast, inexorable pressure seemed to press him downward toward the floor. He hung on to the edge of the sink, swaying on his feet, and when he finally returned to himself, his heart beating hard, he slowly stood up before leaning down again and running cold water on his face for a full sixty seconds.

Upstairs, Potash did his level best to rejoin a conversation his tipsy wife had begun about making synthetic sandalwood, but he himself was no longer drunk in the least. The flare of anxiety had burned it right out of his system. He found himself staring fixedly at the front door of the restaurant for several minutes as if by sheer force of will he could make Janelle materialize out of the night air and run up to his table crying, "My God, John, there was a car crash on the highway and I'd left my cell phone at home!"

When he finally returned his attention to the table, his wife, as if it were the punch line of a long anecdote, was just saying the word *polymerize.* He smiled at her, stood back up and rushed again to the bathroom, where this time he dialed 911. The desk sergeant on call seemed bored by his story and kicked him upstairs along the chain of command to the fraud unit, giving him the number and telling him to call the next day.

After a sleepless night, Potash phoned his old friend Casper Macaleer the first thing next morning. Cas was an ex–college room-mate now wired heart and soul into the Street who, upon hearing him out at length, asked two questions: "John, why didn't you come to me before you made a move of this size?" And: "Did you ever think about why Greenleaf Financial just happens to have a small satellite office in your little pissant town when they only have two or three in the whole country and five in the world?"

Shouting something not entirely coherent in response, Potash hung up, jumped in his SUV and, driving maniacally, arrived ten minutes later at the local offices of Greenleaf Financial. He whipped through the front doors and was halfway across the lobby when he jerked suddenly to a stop like someone whose hips had locked tight.

He'd never talked to the New York office. Slowly, he took his left foot where it was lingering still planted behind him and drew it even with his right. He'd never talked to New York even once. He turned slowly in the space of the lobby, marveling. He'd always be-lieved himself a far-seeing man, but he'd been as blind as a baby, as helpless as a newborn.

He'd just wired the vast majority of his savings into thin air and he'd never talked to New York.

A kind of foul mist clouding his eyes, he got on the nearby eleva-tor. It rose slowly upward, the ping sounded, the door slid open and with a gut-shot heavy feeling he walked down the hallway of suites till he found the door that had formerly led to Greenleaf. Though it still bore the vaguely planetary logo, it was locked tight.

"Lemme guess," said a passing secretary, staring at Potash with a slightly pitying air. "Another person for Greenleaf, right? They're gone, and fast, too."

The girl was continuing to talk to him, but he was barely hearing her. She was saying dully human things like, *They seemed like nice people, but this moving van pulled up, and the next thing I knew the office was locked and they were out of here lickety-split. People were coming by all day yesterday and looking about as unhappy as a person can.*

With a peculiar copper taste in his mouth, he took the elevator back down and walked back through the lobby. He felt like a stick figure in an illustration manual. Slumping nearly in tears on a bench in front of the building, he again dialed Cas, who picked up on the first ring.

"Oh," said Potash softly into the phone, "my God."

"John," shouted Casper, "what happened?"

"I feel like I'm dying, Cas."

There was a silence on the other end, and then Casper, in a low voice, said, "Oh, shit."

"Just like you said, it was a front," Potash croaked. "A front, totally. And so fucking slick and well done that I never thought to talk to New York." Suddenly he felt tears, but they were tears of disappointment at his own stupidity. "I mean," he repeated in a lowered voice, "I never talked to New York, Cas." And then, again, and as if it was the bitterest, saddest admission of defeat, "Not once."

"John," said Cas, simply.

"And now," Potash said, wanting suddenly to tear at his head, stab or gouge himself, "now I don't know what."

"Well, there's procedures," said Casper. "I mean, there are resources."

Potash, breathing heavily, said only, "I'm drowning, Cas."

"John, you've gotta be strong here and think clearly and, I know it's next to impossible, but you've also gotta not get emotional."

Potash let out a sharp, unfiltered shout.

"Like that," said Casper.

"Excuse me, Mr. Potash?"

He opened his eyes, and for a split second, in the perfect hush before sense returned, dwelled happily in the hope that all this had happened to someone else.

"Yes?" he asked groggily.

"Agent Bortz will see you now."

And then he remembered.

"Thank you."

Getting to his feet, Potash followed the receptionist down a long back hallway, where he was ushered into the appropriate office. As he stood a moment on the threshold, his initial impression of the individual who held the last, best hope for his fiscal future was that, in contradistinction to his cow-calling name, Agent Hiram Bortz was a strikingly handsome man.

"Mr. Potash," he said by way of introduction, greeting him across a large, meticulously clean desk, "come in. It seems you fell in with some bad folks."

"You might say," said Potash, walking forward and sitting down while attempting a medium smile of his own.

Bortz, who was in his midthirties, had cropped dark hair, sharp blue eyes and the manner of someone studying you for the fault line in your outlook.

He dropped his eyes to the folder in front of him and squinted for a second. "I won't gild the lily here."

He raised the freezing blue eyes.

"I received your intake complaint a few days ago and have done a little investigation. In the process, I've contacted the U.S. Attorney's Office, Central District, and will be pitching the case to them as a wire fraud later today. If they agree, the two of us would take it up together. Bear in mind that we're looking at a minimum six months before anything happens. Also, let's face it, Mr. Potash, these people are obviously professionals. This wasn't a simple penny-stock scam or a pump and dump, but rather a coordinated and extremely professional effort to wipe you and a group of other, uh, investors out."

Potash, with a lump in his throat, nodded.

"And you should also remember that recovery rates of assets through court actions in cases of large-level fraud of this sort are pretty low."

"Mr. Bortz?"

"Sir?"

"I've been kind of destroyed here. There's gotta be *some* legal recourse."

"Well," Bortz looked at him with an ironic twinkle, "there is a tax break called a Section 165, which will allow you to deduct your loss, but I suspect that's not what you're talking about."

But Potash, deep in his misery, said only, "I keep wondering what I did wrong, why they zeroed in on me."

"That's not really my department," said Bortz, "but let me turn it around for you and ask: Can you think of any obvious way in which you might have made yourself publicly vulnerable—showing off at parties, talking about your nest egg?"

"No, that's not my way."

"Okay. Were there any public announcements regarding your arrival here, anything that might have indicated to a watchful eye that you'd come to invest money in the area?"

"That's the thing. No. I mean, there might have been a small notice somewhere in some educational journal, but my moving here was in no way a public event."

"I see. Well, let me ask you this. Have you been married recently?"

Potash was surprised.

"Married? Well, yes. But what does that . . ."

Bortz leaned his head forward as if to allow Potash to come to his own conclusions. When he didn't, he went on to say, very calmly, "Did you take out an announcement?"

From the center out, Potash felt a slow, burning crumpling feeling.

"Yes," he said.

"Maybe mentioning your relocation to an affluent neighborhood?"

Unable to speak, he simply nodded.

"Real estate transactions," said Bortz, "are public domain."

Ruefully, he recalled Anabella's girlish joy in the wedding announcement, and his own somewhat reluctant participation in something that, in the broadest terms, simply embarrassed him a little. But she'd been having so much fun that he'd gone along with her. As he'd done in so many recent things, overriding his own suspicions in the belief this woman had something to teach him about human nature that his more calculating, cynical self had never before permitted itself, he'd said sure. The fruits of that compliance, a four-color image of the two of them comfortably composed under a grape arbor in Napa, beaming out at the camera with their announcement bannered below, had appeared in the *San Francisco Examiner*. Staring at his shoes, he said softly, "I think I see what you're getting at."

"Indeed," said Bortz, and allowed a pause for the truth to sink in. "As to what you can do now, well, that's entirely up to you. We will, if the case goes forward, move considerable resources into it, rest assured, and do our best to apprehend these people. I can understand that the time frame may not work for you, but that's about all I can tell you."

Potash at this point actually put his face in his hands. When he took them away, the FBI agent was looking at him with a not unkindly expression. He seemed to be thinking.

"Here's what I can't do," Bortz said in a softer voice. "I can't tell you to try to get to her, personally. I can't tell you to hire a PI skilled in such things and try to track her down and confront her with arrest, and maybe attempt to bargain a partial return of the monies in exchange for not pressing charges. I can't tell you I know a person who's been effective at that from time to time, and most of all what I can't do is provide you his name."

Continuing to hold his eye, Bortz slid a card across the table.

"What I *can* tell you," he said, "is that whichever way you go, you're going to have a tough time of it."

"Thank you," Potash said hoarsely.

"Because your girl," said Bortz, "is good."

On the trip home, traffic had abated and he drove on the interstate in a trance, making tiny yanks of the wheel to the right and the left while the landscape gave the impression of being slowly hauled by on either side. After an hour and a half, he left the highway and entered the gently curving roads of his development. Presently, his house appeared around a bend with its calm, tidy proportions, its deep green lawn and beckoning eyelike eaves. It seemed to him just then to be glowing with dumb innocence, like a middle-aged matron receiving guests while being betrayed by her husband in the back room.

He parked and almost immediately saw his wife coming out of the house holding the cordless phone in one hand. Anabella was radiant, her lean body seeming to rise up, up, up, and for a brief, wild second, seeing her there haloed with salvational light, he was certain that she had Janelle Styles on the line and that it had all been a terrible misunderstanding. He was still lurching after this thought when to his dismay he watched her mouth the words *your mother* and extend the phone in his direction.

Of all the words he wanted to hear at this moment, those two ranked near the very bottom. But since his father's death a year earlier, he'd found it simply impossible not to take his mother's calls.

He faked a quick smile at his wife, who still knew nothing about their imminent financial collapse, got out of the car and with a grazing kiss on her lips, retrieved the handset.

"John?"

"Hi, Mom."

"Happy anniversary." Her tone was deadpan.

"It's not for another month," he said.

"I was being proactive."

"How'd you even know?" He was astonished.

"Your wife, Little Miss Sunshine, told me. But isn't every day an anniversary out at Camp Cosmic?"

Sarcasm was one of her main weapons. Her belief was that his town was a hippy-dippy Aquarian paradise filled with complacent millionaires, and that she and she alone knew the harsh truth of how the world was made. He loved her, and yet felt very happy to be half a world away from her.

"Ha-ha," he said miserably.

"So how's life?"

Her timing was uncanny. His whole life she had called at weak moments, stumblings, setbacks of all kinds.

"Just dandy," he said.

"Are you sure?"

"What's up, Mom?"

"What, a mother can't ask her son a simple question?"

He said nothing for a moment.

"Listen," she said, "and for at least the third time. Your father's stone is being unveiled next week, and it's important that you be here."

"Of course I'll be there. We already spoke about it."

"It's very important," she said, ignoring his utterance.

He could hear her voice thickening.

"I mean it's the least we can do," she said, her voice thickening further.

"Mom," he said.

"It's a beautiful stone," she said, now in full flow. Potash was used to these tacks and spins of feeling. She lived in an ongoing mood best described as the Stentorian Memorial, in which people she'd ignored while alive became in death touchstones of deep grief.

"I'm sure," he said.

"But don't worry about me!" she burst out.

"Mom," he said again.

His mother was overweight, and the stertor of her breath on the phone as she breathed in and out for a few seconds was like a piece of paper being repeatedly crumpled in his ear.

"Even a little bit," she whispered, and then hung up.

CHAPTER TEN

At age sixteen, she met Randy Patterson. He had flaming sideburns, tight jeans, and a small, beautiful head. From the start, she found it impossible not to be amazed by the way the air around her body fitted into the air around his. Everyone noticed. It was what "natural" meant. They were natural together. They went to concerts and made out backstage. They walked on the Atlantic City boardwalk and watched waves arrive from all over the world. With their arms around each other, they felt docked, like spaceships. Even better, they understood each other's smallest mannerisms. He could cock an eyebrow and signal an avalanche of judgment about to fall, or tilt his head a mere ironic inch and it would be as if he was whispering his thoughts directly into her ear. He worked as a line cook at a Denny's and played bass in a band called Gridlock.

One afternoon several months after they'd officially begun going steady, Randy was especially excited because, he explained, he had a "big fat stonking secret" that he was gonna show her later that day.

That same evening, at dusk, they were parked and making out in his Pontiac Firebird Trans Am when he grabbed her by the shoulders.

"You ready?" he asked.

"Guess so."

With a nod, he started the car and drove the two of them to a Walgreens and then around back. The powerful engine idled like someone tapping an empty can with a hammer. He turned off the car.

"Here we go," he said, and got out of the car with a wink.

Out the window, she watched Randy foraging in the Dumpster. He pulled something up, looked quickly around, stuffed it under his peacoat, and then got back in the car.

"What's that?" she asked.

Slowly, like someone pulling back a magic curtain, he revealed an assortment of pill bottles in a plastic bag.

"Are you sick?" she asked, thrilled.

He gave his special wide-eyed look, threw back his head and howled like a coyote. "Hell, yeah," he cried, "but not in the way you're thinking! I got a friend who works as a janitor there. We got it all worked out. He's into pharmaceuticals, and he tosses the stuff out with the trash and then I swing by and vwalah, baby. What we don't use, we sell."

"Wow."

Back home, she had recently discovered something in a drawer of her father's dresser. It was a note from a girl. It was on pink stationery. It said, "You're just the dearest man I've ever met, and no one makes me laugh harder." It was the kind of handwriting in which all the letters looked like they were swollen with gas. She said nothing at the time. She didn't even think much of it. But two nights later, in her diary, she solemnly wrote, "I've come to the conclusion that in life, virginity is silly, and in love, blow jobs are not enough." The next day, she stole a leopard thong from J.J. Newberry.

She wanted to fuck him. It didn't have to be in one of the perfect large beachside homes of the soap opera stars whose antics her mother now watched constantly while lying in bed. It didn't have to be in the many-roomed, ivy-covered mansions of her books. It could as easily be in his Trans Am parked along the beach. There was a cove near Race Point where you felt lifted right out of the world. She wanted to go to the quiet closet of that cove. She wanted to give him her body. When he played in his band, she used to watch his hands as they ranged along the frets and imagine his nakedness somehow as an extension of the sounds he made onstage.

"Take this," he said, holding a pill up.

"What'll it do?" She wasn't frightened, only curious.

"Nothing, really. It'll just make you feel free."

She smiled at him.

"Sure," she said.

An hour later she was sitting in the car at the beach thinking how the waves were like hands as they individually unfisted against the sand and how peaceful it would be to go to the bottom of the ocean and just lie there being massaged by those long green fingers. She was thinking that the secret of the universe was that everything lived apart from everything else but was connected by the bright, living fluid of eyesight. And in eyesight there were no failures or winters or famines. Instead, everything was perfect and extended forever in all directions like daylight. His face of a beautiful living creature was drawing very close. His eyes were glistening with tears. Her own eyes were filling too, even as she felt her body suddenly leave her bones, fly through the air and gather in a far-off tree, where it sat there looking peacefully out at the world, like a cat.

They went steady for a year, during which time they began having sex. It was uncomfortable at first, and she was faintly disappointed. But it seemed to mean so much to him. When they eventually drifted *apart, she told herself that she was no longer a girl but a woman in possession of a new illumination: that sex had a way of allowing men to believe they were permanently in control. But that once you got it over with, the far more important business of life lay waiting, and because they were distracted by their recent performance, men could easily—like large machines pivoting smoothly on ball bearings—be rotated at will.*

Six months before college, with mementos of Randy now moved to the back of the closet in the slow sideways crawl of objects through her room and into storage in boxes and on high shelves, she took a solemn vow of sex. Immediately afterward, with a completely impassive look on her face, she began fucking as many boys as possible. She fucked them in cars. She fucked them in the living rooms of their parents' houses. With cramps in her legs, she fucked them standing up in the supply closets of school. She told herself she was storing up important experience. She told herself she was experimenting her way toward what would eventually be mastery.

She felt nothing, nothing at all. She was utterly numb. One evening around this time, she took a knife and cut herself slowly and repeatedly on the arm and it was like opening a window in the house and letting the bad air out of her own body.

Then she matriculated at Smith College, which resembled a British country mansion with its pavilions and lawns and winding flagstone paths. She took a full roster of English courses and dated sporadically and with no particular satisfaction among the widest, deepest talent pool of boys she'd ever seen. She had two lesbian flings, but her interest quickly flagged. Though she had a private off-campus room and kept mostly to herself, she sometimes spent time with a group of black-clad girls who read everything and knew everyone and found common cause in pronouncing themselves bored to tears.

At the end of her second year, her mother died. The funeral was held on a warm spring day. The smell of the grass was suffocating. The gravesite was flanked on every side by mild elevations. These gave the impression that one slid downhill into waiting death. A scattering of relatives had flown in from all over the country. Minister Cartwright led the service, and then her father, swaying erratically, read a eulogy describing the "sacred compact and Christian joy" of marriage. Margot said nothing at the funeral. She solemnly accepted the condolences of relatives and filled their glasses at the reception held in their living room. Tears tracked down her cheeks, and she watched them fall. Experimentally, she tried to imagine that she would never see her mother again in life but couldn't conceive of it. Then that night, back in college, she did two lines of powerful coke and blew her bearded English professor, a man by the name of Neil Walsh who knew more about certain poems of Walt Whitman than any man alive.

At the beginning of her third year in college, her major was still undeclared. But in early September the phone rang in her room. Her father was on the other end and told her that he'd been fired from his job in the public defender's office. Stephen McMahon the city ombudsman was a low-life gutter-crawling Judas who would rue the day he'd brought down the last honest man in Massachusetts. He'd worked his heart out for the people and now the people, in the person of this vile cur, had killed him dead. It's a good thing your dear mother isn't around to see this.

She heard the ice cubes tinkling in his glass as he began to cry. When he recovered his composure and blew his nose, he told her how sorry he was about what this meant for her.

*When she asked what **did** this mean for her, he told her he'd been effectively blackballed, and how the hell did she think a fifty-six-year-*

old out-of-work lawyer would find a job? The best thing, he added, would be for her to take a loan out for the coming semester.

She wasn't certain she'd heard him right and asked for clarification.

"Honey," he said, "we're broke."

The next day, she made an appointment with her guidance counselor and over his objections changed her concentration to a split literature/business focus, signing up for courses in marketing, accounting and finance. In the meantime, to console herself, she decided to blame her father for everything.

CHAPTER ELEVEN

He'd accepted her dinner invitation. Why had he accepted? His life was replete. He loved his wife. Why was he sitting at this restaurant dressed in his worsted wool suit, while enjoying the pressure in the air of her glance on his face; her lit, roving, happy glance?

"You were saying?" she was asking. Her face glowed under the subtle mask of its makeup.

He took a bead on himself. All the internal pressure seals were holding just fine. "I was saying," he said, "that the way I got into it was through studying psychology, at first, because, it simply seemed the kind of thing you were supposed to study if you wanted to know the way the mind worked."

"Right," she said, "but what led you to *that*, I'm asking?"

"I was just a curious kid, I guess."

"Well, that doesn't surprise me in the least."

Their food was served. He tried, again, to quell his potentially bolting nerves. He was simply out of practice. He couldn't remember the last time he'd been alone with a woman in an extended social situation, sanctioned by his wife—even if his wife hadn't understood exactly what he was doing, and had airily said, as he was leaving, "Have fun, darling."

"But there's something so boring about psychology," he started to say when she interrupted him.

"Don't talk," she said.

"Why not?"

"Because I want to watch you eat."

"Beg your pardon?" A mottled blush, beginning at the breastbone, was spreading outward over his chest.

"Think of it as revenge for you calling me up onstage that day. Besides, I'm taking you out tonight so I can do what I want."

"Can you now," he said in a low voice.

But instead of answering him, she merely kept chewing while studying his face for a long moment.

"You have a sensual upper lip," she said, "but a real pleasure-denying lower one. And you have, Mr. Billings, a pronounced filtrum."

The filtrum, or groove between the base of the nose and lips, was one of the classic tells of sexual desire—as she well knew. He stared at her while a wave of confused heat roiled through his head even as, outwardly, he gave no sign of his discomfiture in the least and continued to cut his meat with small composed sawing motions.

"Are you flirting with me?" he asked.

"I'm not sure," she said, and laughed an open laugh, one of the most open laughs he'd ever heard from this tactically brilliant girl, "but if I decide to, I'll let you know."

She had a beautiful head of newly cut and dyed short blond hair, which was parted on one side like a boy, and put into fresh relief the deep, symmetrical sensuality of her features. From these, in regular bursts, fusillades of saucy mischievous looks were flying in his direction.

"Let's return," he said, clearing his throat lengthily, "to your previous question about how I got my start. I'm not sure if there was a single event, but when I think back on it, I can remember that my parents knew this couple who they would have over every once in a while for dinner. I might have been only a kid at the time, but I could still see plain as day that the wife hated the weakness of the husband, and that the husband was grossed out by the loudness of the wife, and that below the polite party chatter there was this sound track of dark, muffled sounds the two of them made at each other, which was the way they really felt. I could see it, and I could hear it too, those sounds, like dying animals make, beneath the polite conversation. The thing was, I thought everyone else did too. I thought everyone heard the secret sound track. I thought that everyone saw how people form a little mask to protect themselves, and a little story in which they're the hero, and how the mask rides the story like a horse into the sunset of their own minds."

He realized that in his concentrated effort at recall, he had been addressing what face readers called the lateral catch, that is, that space right below her right eye. He raised his eyes to hers.

"On the other hand," he said, "no one is a devil if you listen to them for long enough."

Her finger was lazily circling the rim of her wineglass.

"Then what?" she asked.

"How do you mean?"

"How did you get from there"—she stabbed a long polished fingernail onto the linen tablecloth and drew it toward her with the rising rasp of a zipper opening—"to here?"

The science of touch is called haptics. He'd always been particularly sensitive to touch, even a touch that was entirely implied like the one he'd just witnessed of her finger on the tablecloth. He could feel something, an aroused signal moving through yards of sluggish abdominal flesh.

"Practice," he said with a wink, and before she could even respond, he added, abruptly, "Follow my elbow, please."

"What?"

He relished her confusion as he reached up to deliberately scratch his nose.

"My elbow," he said. "Are you following where it's pointing?"

"Yes."

"Do you see that woman?"

"In the blue pantsuit, whose back is toward us?"

"Yes. We passed directly in front of her while walking in and we even crossed glances with her, the two of us."

"I remember, yes."

"Read her, please."

She made a laughing, outraged sound of disbelief, but when she saw he was serious, she grew serious as well. She shut her eyes, spread her hands on the table, and tilted her head, concentrating hard, her brow wrinkling with the effort.

"Wavy hairline," she said, her eyes fluttering slightly, "with some particular disturbance at about age fourteen, thin lower and slightly thicker upper lips, and the . . . the moneybag pouches, the extra plump spaces on the lower cheeks around the mouth." She raised her eyes to his, triumphant. "Reserves of energy," she said. "The gal is probably tireless."

"Check." He enjoyed slipping back into the lightly sexualized choreography of instruction. "And what else?"

"Oooh, you're evil. Okay." Again she shut her eyes and lowered her head, slightly, so that he could see the way the part in her hair wound in a French curve around the top of her skull.

"I'm picking up," she said, "a cleft chin. Which would mean a substantial ego, and likes to perform."

"Ah, very good," he was genuinely satisfied. "And?"

"The ears," she said, after a moment, "are large and are riding low on the head. That would make her a thoughtful and deliberate type, most likely. Oh, and another thing, the glabellar fold between the eyes. She has a deep, deep crease there—some blocks of a sort maybe in the male side of her personality."

"I'm impressed," he said softly. "You do good work."

She looked up at him, smiling brilliantly.

"I'm only as good as my teacher," she said.

She reached her hand across the table and touched the top of his own hand. Nearly instantly, his ears began to burn.

"Thank you," he said calmly, not giving away a thing.

CHAPTER TWELVE

Two days before flying east to see his mother, Potash's stepsons threw a "celebration" for him. According to statistical opinion, he'd entered their life too late for him to have an easy ride as paternal stand-in. They were already twelve and thirteen upon his arrival and fully embarked on that loud, demonstrative phase of adolescence that is as close to a finished human being as an exploded diagram of a car is to an idling Rolls-Royce. Yet what the statisticians couldn't know was that Potash had a secret weapon. As an educator, he'd spent the formative years of his adulthood "getting inside" of children, precisely the age of his new boys. He knew the lingo, the signs, the head fakes of being fourteen like very few adults—so he told himself—on earth.

On that particular day, Potash was returning, fatefully enough, from the bank, where he'd just overseen the arrival of a "bridge loan" of $25,000 from Cas in New York. This was useful both to keep the piranhas of his many autopays at bay and to buy him a little more time to sort out his mess without his wife knowing.

It was his wife whose plum-shaped derriere he now saw as he

drove up the driveway. Wearing shorts, she was gardening with her headphones on—root-feeding the hydrangeas at that very moment. Rather than get out of the car, Potash parked, and tried to offset his maintenance-level bad mood by sitting there and consciously enumerating to himself—in the face of overwhelming evidence to the contrary—the good fortune of his life. This was an exercise recommended by his men's group as a way, they claimed, of laddering one's self nearly physically into a state of satori.

He began, as he was supposed to, with the local, or he supposed, Local. This he did by dwelling on the outlying suburban grid of houses, artfully screened one from the other through small trompe l'oeil wilderness settings, where lean, smart people were returning home from work in their low-pollution cars and sustainable light-rail conveyances. Many of them wore clothes made of recycled plastic bottles and employed personal skin and hair-care products derived from low-carbon footprint processes. They drank shade-grown coffee and ate foods rich in monophytomers and glyconutrients. Progressive on all the important questions, they drove life toward a kinder, cleaner, more humanly scaled future.

These were his people. He belonged among them. Somehow or another, he'd aligned the energies of his life to arrive at their golden summit in the pecking order of destiny. Had any citizens in history ever been more deliciously replete in their existence? Had any, through the weightless clairvoyance of connectivity, ever been more conscious of the planetary fragility of life—and more grateful for what they had?

He got out of the car, uncertain whether or not all this internal smoke-blowing had helped, and noticed his wife, attracted by the movement, standing up and slipping off her headphones. She sauntered over to kiss him hello, and then stood a moment smiling upward at him, while the sun lay in bright little cups on her cheek-bones. Brimful of vitality, she sometimes made Potash feel as if he'd grown up entirely underground, like a mushroom.

"You smell like car," she said, with a laugh. "Come inside, honey. The boys have done something special for the occasion."

"The boys? What'd they do? What occasion?"

"You know them, they won't tell me a thing. I'm just their mother."

She drew him by the hand through the front door. The first thing he noticed was that the living room shades were drawn, creating a shadowy atmosphere, and that through the stereo speakers poured loud, breathy noises like those of a theme-park haunted house.

"Sit down," said a freshly adolescent deep voice through the speakers, "and behold."

As Potash sat, with Anabella alongside him on the couch, a slide was projected on a far wall. It was a photograph of their home taken from a hundred yards away and slightly below. The result, remark-ably professional, was to give their split-level a beautiful, "house on a hill" look.

"Inside," said the voice, "the new man of the house sleeps the sleep of the just."

Where, Potash wondered, did his older stepson come up with this stuff? Most of the time he was occupied reading books about gory alien dismemberment with an occasional stab into Tom Clancy for some flag-waving crypto-fascism. But the source of his extensive vocabulary remained a mystery.

The slide now shining on the wall showed Potash porpoised on his side in sleep. His mouth was open. His hair, normally combed carefully over his bald spot, was spun around his head in satellitic disarray. His gut stuck out. Held warmly in his, his wife's hand tightened.

"It stirs."

In this next shot, he was lying on his back, his mouth open like that of a dying old person in the midst of agonal breathing.

"In the mirror, the creature stares at itself."

Shot from what must have been a tiny pin-camera concealed near the shower tubing, a slide was projected of Potash, baggy eyed and palpably hungover, wearing only a towel and staring at the mirror.

"It checks itself for hostile bodies."

A finger was now in his mouth, pushing his lip way over to one side as if to palp his gums for tenderness. Subsequent shots in front of that same mirror would show him yawning, scratching under his armpits, and then making a Magoo-ish expression into the glass, as if daring it to answer back. Finally, like most of the rest of the world upon awakening, he was seen brushing his teeth.

"I wasn't aware," he said softly to his wife, "I was under surveillance, nor that the 'celebration' would be a disguised takedown."

"You're not offended, are you?"

She saw the whole thing through a forgiving maternal lens. It was high jinks. It was charming tomfoolery. She had a generous, open nature, and he told himself that she simply didn't understand people like him, who worked from the ego, with the ego's sullen strictures, its sour smell.

"Of course not," he lied.

Ten months earlier, not long after his arrival on the scene in California, he and Anabella and the kids had gone to see one of those films in which cable optics have been inserted into the formerly private parts of men and women to observe the secret gestational processes of life at work: fertilization, pregnancy and birth. Potash had smilingly entered the theater, but as he watched the fizzing little whip-tailed sperm swarming the large, helpless moon of the egg, he was overcome with a remorseful sense of exclusion from his wife's body so large it drove him from the theater and out to the hall, where, three floors up, he quite seriously pondered jumping from the balcony. Instead, childless himself, he sobbed uncontrollably at the thought he would never sire children with her. This, he thought, is love, what it does, how it deranges, and in the guise of passion, how it destroys.

The boys were coming forward to take a bow. They were deeply pleased with themselves. They relished giving him the business while remaining protected within their roles of just being kids. This seemed to Potash patently unfair, like a preteen committing murder and then walking. A friend had once told him that the main business of teenagers was to destroy their parents; that this was what being a teenager *was*. Potash was applauding the little murderers, thinking, *It's only the beginning,* when his phone buzzed. It was the PI he'd contacted at the suggestion of Hiram Bortz, texting to ask him if they could advance their appointment by a day, to this afternoon.

He looked up from his phone to see the boys, Louis and Terry, now standing directly before him, awaiting his response. Early in his career, for three summers in a row, he'd counseled hard-core middle-school truants and had learned to keep his realer feelings to himself when faced with even the most flagrant provocation.

"Pretty funny, guys," he said casually, and held out his fist.

They individually fist-bumped him back, giggling with pleasure while his wife made love-eyes at him for his big, understanding heart, and below the happy scene he struggled, as he had for four days straight, to understand how a man with everything in the world going for him could have so successfully buried himself alive. Dropping his eyes back to his lap, he only dimly heard the children and his wife laughing in an overflow of family feeling as he texted back, "Roger that. The sooner the better."

CHAPTER THIRTEEN

When college was over, the black-clad girlfriends she'd had for four years scattered individually to their summer islands and boats, moving on from there to graduate schools in England and the Ivy League. Two weeks after graduation, she took a job in Northampton, working for the Klein-Newsome art gallery. She'd ended college with perfect grades, a few acquaintances, several ex-lovers, sixty thousand dollars of debt and no prospects. Her father had by now drunk himself into a complaisant torpor and did paperwork three afternoons a week for his former assistant.

And so, while she regularly received postcards from Positano, and Cinque Terre, and Paros, Greece, which she carefully tacked in a gay little arch above the mirror of her bathroom in a rented room, her days were mainly spent watching herself impersonate a wholesome just-graduated college girl. For hours, she wandered each day at work amid watercolors of daisies, calla lilies and nasturtiums spilling over rock gardens, while saying to clients, "These are all by local artists," and "That series is very popular as wedding presents," and "Expectant mothers find that sea scenes are deeply calming."

One afternoon in early September, with the town again flooded with students, she had an illumination. A father had come in with his daughter to buy a painting for her dorm room. The father was a handsome, well-dressed man with a mantle of gray hair and fine hands. He looked every inch the part of an Ivy League English professor. His daughter had about her the wholesomeness of a girl who'd played field hockey and aced Shakespeare at some country school with high educational standards and a Quaker-based curriculum.

Of course she loathed the girl; to a certain extent the father too. But later that night, while alone in her rented room, a searing rage at her father came over her, followed shortly by waves of tears so violent that her stomach began to cramp. On impulse, she shut off the television, lay down in bed fully clothed, put her sleep mask on, and thought hard for about a half hour. When she got up, taking off her mask, she had made up her mind.

The next morning, she called in sick to work and caught an early morning bus out of Northampton. Her father's house was two hours away, and during the ride, she meditated on the plan that had come to her wholly formed while lying in bed with her eyes covered. Years earlier, in an effort to evade detection, her father had begun paying his multiplying numbers of "girlfriends" in disbursements of $200 and $300 out of a bewildering variety of accounts, and he had never consolidated them. To hear him say it, he was "flat broke," but she knew he had many small sums of money scattered around various banks in a galaxy of mostly inactive accounts. These accounts would be her target.

Everything went exactly as planned. She'd phoned her father from the bus to make sure he'd be at work. A taxi took her to the deserted house. Once inside, she moved with a dowser's intuition in a widening spiral through the rooms with their various caches and hiding places till she found the object of her desire: a wooden box containing a collection of ancient flapping checkbooks. From there it was but a signature forged, a friendly handshake with the elderly teller at the local credit union where her family had banked for years and she was heading back to campus with a thousand dollars in her bag and a cushion of several weeks or months before her father figured out what had happened.

As the bus on giant tires advanced over winding sunset roads she told herself she felt like a seed being borne on a river to a sacred patch of soil. This she would make flower into a plant of deep importance. The secrecy of her mission lent it power. The illegality of it lent it extra life. She felt calmer and more centered than she could remember feeling in years. Shit, she thought, staring out the window, I could get used to this.

"Get used to what?" Dan France now said directly into her ear.

She opened her eyes.

"What?" she asked, slowly.

"You were muttering to yourself in your sleep," he said, clearly very pleased with himself.

"I—"

"I couldn't make much out, but I did hear 'get used to this.'"

"Oh, God," she said softly.

"No worries!" He laughed delightedly. He was out of his normal suit, and dressed casually in chinos and a T-shirt. He moved around her bed, raised on the balls of his feet, and smiled with his catlike lips.

"So, how's tricks?"

"Fine," she said automatically, and then with an effort, correcting herself: "Tired, actually. Very tired."

"That's good that you're tired. Before you were so tired you didn't even know you were tired."

She yawned.

"Tired is as tired does," she said, "or something."

His smile was steady; it seemed as if fed from some internal spring.

"You wanna take a ride?" he asked.

"I don't under—"

"A little spin around the grounds?"

"What are you talking about?"

"Just this." He stood up and retrieved from behind him a wheelchair, which he brought around smartly to the side of the bed.

"Seriously?"

"I've already cleared it with the powers that be."

An hour later, he was pushing her slowly along the flagstone paths. The wheels crackled over the leaves. The daylight, sunshine, and smells flowed across her senses with shocking vividness.

"The world," she said softly, "is kinda intense."

"After your 'accident,' almost anything would probably feel like that."

"Why do you do that?"

"What?"

"Say the word like that, 'accident.'"

"Ah." He stopped pushing and came around the front of the wheelchair and squatted in front of her in a way that made his head look unnaturally large and detailed.

"Well, that's the million-dollar question, isn't it, whether this was an accident, or not."

She merely stared at him.

"I'm here on a kinda two-track mission," he said, and held his hands again up in the air. "The professional," he said, wiggling his right hand, "goes forward with the investigation. The personal"—he wiggled his left—"well . . ."

He dropped his hands.

"I think you're a very special person," he said. "So sue me."

She looked at him. "Is that the way detectives talk?" she said slowly.

He laughed again. "See?" he said. "That's what I'm talking about."

A chrome tanker truck, crossing a distant bridge, threw a glowing star of light across a mile of air and directly into her eye. Didn't everyone understand how smashingly violent the world was?

"Listen," he said, "in all seriousness, I have something for you."

"What's that?" she asked, as with great care he placed a blank pad of paper in her lap.

Instead of answering, he drew a sharpened number 2 pencil from his pocket and closed her fingers around it in a way that made a hot and sour tingle run through her body.

"I want you to draw a face," he said.

"A face? What kind of face?"

Sometimes she could feel the place where it used to be, wit; a blank space of bumpy air. But it was coming back.

"What kind of face?" she repeated.

"Any kind," he said, and then in response to her evident incomprehension, he said, "Your memory has been impaired by what happened to you, but I have a real interest in knowing more about the people who've been around you recently. And drawing the last face you can remember seeing might just furnish us some clues."

He leaned forward into the smooth, sparkling, incredibly interesting air.

"Okay?" he asked.

"Okay," she said, feeling it coming back, fast. It was an old story. She had once been so good at it. It had once been so dependable. Now she remembered. You put the feelings in the one side, and out came

the hard, specific things from the other. Sex, interest, and money especially. Big jangling showers of money. Delicious rivers of it, winding among sparkling far banks of commodities. Those black-clad friends of hers of college had almost all of them married rich or been rich to start with. But what had she done? Why hadn't she gotten rich? Or had she? Dan France was nodding at her like he knew something and wasn't telling.

Or had she?

CHAPTER FOURTEEN

Lawrence managed to close out the dinner without anything untoward taking place, but at the end of the evening, as he was saying good night, she surprised him by pressing swiftly against him with an openmouthed kiss on the lips that shocked for how it caused him to linger there, caught in a thick buzzing confusion, until a sharp signal of a sort shuddered between them. At which point, satisfied, she drew away and looked at him, her face gleaming. An average person would have only assumed her happy and replete. But tiny signs of asymmetric contraction around the eyes and mouth alerted him to the ambiguity of her pleasure. Other emotions were leaking out across her face; darker, colder emotions moving particularly across the left or "personal" side of her features. But before he could come to any further conclusions, she patted him on the cheek and spun swiftly away, her heels clopping down the night street.

They had set a lesson appointment for five days hence. As chance would have it, those next days were dense with the bureaucratic side of his business. In reality, he didn't mind. Lawrence wasn't a natural showman; he'd had to train himself over the years in the inflationary gestures and exaggerations of the stage. He'd become good at it, but it remained something willed and only marginally enjoyed. That being the case, he found these administrative operations actually a kind of relief. Fine-tuning future seminars, laying out schedules, checking on his assistant's availability, and doing everything possible to ensure that the machine known as Lawrence Billings, LLC, ran forward as smoothly and uneventfully as possible was part of the busywork of life. He didn't mind it.

By degrees, he also found himself extra attentive to his wife in this period. He took her out to dinner; he laughed with emphatic animation at her jokes, and upon her return from her book club, feigned deep interest in the discussion. In bed, at night, he rubbed her feet, her temples, her face with the calendula oil she loved. During the night itself, he sometimes felt himself half consciously hunting for her in the bed like a nocturnal creature sensitive only to variations of warmth and chill. Fresh, only partly guilty erotic impulses overwhelmed him from time to time. She was receptive, and a new season of feeling rolled through their marriage.

And why, he asked himself, *shouldn't it?* He adored his wife's solidity, her serene power. She took up space with definitive emphasis. Her hips were large, her breasts were full and her heart, which he sometimes thought of as literally heart-shaped, included in its curves a beautiful breadth of care for plants, animals, justice, and himself most of all. But his feelings were given a twist by his new sense of a terrible fated terminality to everything. When she turned abruptly from a chair to stand up, he now feared she might fall. Slightly overweight people of middle age overtaxed the levers of their bodies on a regular basis and broke things. When she drew a long knife out of the drawer to chop something, he saw her slipping dramatically and ending up transfixed and wriggling like a fish on the shank. Burglars lay in wait and rushed in and hit people on the head. Planes broke open in the sky; cars swerved off the road because of the fatigue of tiny elbows of metal and killed all aboard. The world was a series of cocked guns and ticking probabilities.

Margot called twice; he didn't pick up, and she left no message.

On the fifth day, as planned, he was at his office and waiting for her. He had successfully disguised his excitement by displacing it into a fresh awareness of the cheap construction of his suite. When would he ever get the crappy particleboard walls repainted and the moldy bathroom tiles regrouted? And what about that new T1 line he was forever mulling over? Could he simply move on it?

A brisk little knocking on the glass panel of the office interrupted his reverie.

"Who is it?" he called out, knowing full well.

She made a dramatic stage entrance, pushing one long leg forward in front of the vestibule, touching the point of her sandaled toe to the floor and then rolling it forward to slide her leg into the room up to the thigh. It was campy, high school theater, obviously crude, but it worked. He was intrigued.

"Come in," he said calmly.

She slid the rest of herself into view and took a bow. "Good morning!"

She was dressed in black leggings, a tiny pouf skirt and a fitted black top. Her curves were on display, and her blond hair had been cropped short and freshly gelled.

"Good morning, Margot," he said. "You look very . . . ."—he searched for the right word—"sleek."

"Thank you."

"You're welcome."

She was sitting down, shucking her laptop out of its case, straightening her back and lifting her face to him. He was staring back at her with his eyesight concentrated especially on her smiling mouth. People had no idea what an encyclopedia of information the human smile was. As he often explained to students, the key diagnostic trait of the fraudulent smile was the zero engagement of the muscles around the eyes, and he searched hers for a moment.

"How've you been?" she asked casually.

"Just fine," he said, "very busy. You?"

"How have I been?" She seemed delighted by the question. "What's the word for better than great?" she asked.

"I don't know. Sublime?"

"It's the work, Lawrence. I've just been on this high about it. It's like those people who after being deaf their whole lives get a . . . coch . . . a cocky . . ."

"A cochlear implant?"

"And suddenly their world opens wide?"

"I like the analogy."

"It's like I walk out into the street and I look at people with this kind of second sight or x-ray vision. I can see the bitch a mile away and make evasive maneuvers. I can see the third-rate seducer with his mind in the gutter from before his first crappy come-on. It's a revelation."

"For some people it really can be that." Suddenly he felt moved to talk about himself. "I've always hoped that in addition to everything else, the work would help enlarge people's vision, give them a wider perspective in life generally. It's not simply looking for ways to get ahead; it's about reading humanity, the book of life." He paused, contracting back. "Not to get too overwrought about it."

She was smiling at him again. He'd noticed before that she had the kind of eyes, typically seen in the Asian world, which appear overfull of liquid. He suddenly felt the need to anchor things in the professional. "And your homework for this week?" he asked. "Did you find it useful?"

"When you love the material, it's all useful."

"Right answer!" he said with a grin. "You feel like giving me a recap?"

"You bet."

Biting her inner lip, she opened her tabbed loose-leaf notebook. From upside down, he observed her pages covered with handwriting whose leftward slant indicated a desire for emotional concealment, while bearing the large letter loops of someone sensitive to criticism.

"Let's begin with touch," she said, raising her eyes to his before lowering them. "It's the mother of all sales drivers. In fact, research at the Cornell School of Hotel Administration—"

"Thank you," he interrupted her.

"For?" She looked up, startled.

"Remembering the correct attribution," he said, "that's all."

She made a kind of downward, bosomful nod of the head, said, "Sure," and then went on, "research indicated that the tips of servers went up distinctly when servers touched the arms of diners. Let's see if I can remember the details."

She looked over his head and squinted into the distance in an effort at recollection. "Average tips increased 20 percent when they were touched on the shoulder, I think it was, and 35 percent when they were touched twice on the hand."

All it had been was a kiss, he was thinking; a brief, if intense little clasp of the lips. And yet somehow she'd frontloaded the entirety of her eros into that moment. How had she done that?

"Exactly right," he said.

"In fact, touch"—she was now looking at him appraisingly—"is currently understood to be a key hidden commercial factor. The work done by Fortwell—"

But he'd zoned out, and unusually for him, had stopped listening. He was instead remembering that morning, at age forty-one, when he'd reached up to scratch his own ear and been amazed by the thinness of the lobe. It was as if, unbeknownst to him, the fluids of his body had been traitorously draining away while he slept. For the next hour he'd explored his body with his hands, pinching skin and fat, testing for the places where old age was making its inroads. *This,* he thought, watching her without hearing, *is what makes men greedy for young women—the promise of somehow recuperating that initial plump alacrity of flesh.*

She was saying, "The feet, because they're connected to the limbic system, are the classic autonomic tells, and the Chinese say . . ."

"That's enough," he said. She cocked an interrogative eyebrow.

"I, I think it's time we clear something up," he said.

"Okay, sure. What did you have in mind?"

He felt a reckless, vaulting energy pushing him forward to make a clean breast of things.

"I want us to feel relaxed in our roles," he said. "I enjoy teaching you and mentoring you. But I think it's important to stress that that's all I am, your teacher."

"Good . . . because I've always needed a teacher, and you're just the best at what you do."

Her smile widened, becoming apparently more real. As he'd ex-

plained to his students, many of the muscles of the face were pur-
pose-built for certain emotions, like grief, and could not be activated
fraudulently. But a small group of people were able to fire these muscles independent of their feelings. They were rare, but they existed.

"Thank you," he said.

"And now can *I* say something?"

He nodded his head.

"If I sometimes overstep my bounds, then please understand
what I'm doing in that context as enthusiasm, really. And no more."

"I'm glad for that," he said, feeling increasingly solid in his position. "And I very much appreciate it."

"Oh, goodie."

"Right," he said, "and you should know that while I find you
very attractive"—he paused a second, nodding—"that simply is not
the kind of thing I do."

"Got it." Her eyes were bright. "Oh, and what is *that*?"

"That?" He stopped nodding. Perhaps he'd gone too far.

"Uh, have . . . relations with students," he said.

Her smile widened further. "I so *totally* understand"—she
leaned forward as if to impart a confidence—"and I'm so *totally* in
support of that."

"Well . . . great," he said with an effort.

"And you know what?"

"What?"

"I just think you're the coolest guy for saying so!" And here she
gave a shake of her head, with its cropped furze of blond hair; toss-
ing it like a horse does, with a big lunging motion of the neck, and
as he watched, something in his chest turned over with an incom-
plete motion and he said softly, "Okay."

Then she reached out and touched him again. It was just a touch on the arm, but he somehow seemed to feel it ringing like a struck bell in his body.

"Yet you seem sad," she said.

"Do I?"

"Yes, and I just want you to understand that I'm here for anything you need from me. If you never want to see me again, I'll understand. If you want to tell me a joke, I'll laugh. If you wanna give me a chaste little kiss, I'll probably kiss you back. I love what you're bringing to my life, Lawrence, but I don't want to be a burden, even a little."

"You're a . . . dear," he said, and heard how quaint and even auntish was the phrase. And it was at that moment, for the very first time, that Lawrence Billings felt old. He'd felt mature before; he'd felt accomplished; he'd felt at midcareer, midpoint, midlife before. But at the moment, beached on the sound of that word *dear*, he simply felt dusty.

She leaned toward him; she entered his personal space. He was feeling his own thoughts turning slow, syrupy. In the voice of a running-down record, he was saying to himself, *I am a solid husband. I am a man at the exact center of his life.*

"Maybe not just sad, but pensive too," she said, and he felt the entire swirl of time through the room, like smoke, thickening. *Unable not to,* he reached out to her. His mind would attach itself to that phrase from here on, riding forward in a gathering mass of nonaccountability. *Unable not to,* he drew her toward him. Seen from up close, her eyes sparkled with an unearthly mineral fire. Her perfume enclosed him like a room within a room. *Unable not to,* he kissed her, and gratefully drew her closer still, and she put her strong tongue in his mouth, and then began nuzzling him along the neck with fine bites. *Unable not to,* he floated free of his itching, arguing, contradicting mind, and became a simple body again, potent and limber, and at that moment in time, he no longer knew who he was, and couldn't have cared less.

CHAPTER FIFTEEN

You didn't miss it till it was gone, Potash thought, winging his way back east, to his mother's. From his window seat, he watched as puffy, dreaming sierras of cloud slid silently by below the airplane. You took it cheerfully for granted over the years, he thought, and you came to see it somewhat like water pouring from the tap, or the hugeness of electricity trickling dependably from the wall. Then, when it was removed, you couldn't believe how much of the previous version of yourself became stuck, dry, and chalky, and how a certain gliding comfort you'd believed your birthright was only the emollient effect of dollars in your life.

The clouds opened up, revealing a dun stretch of earth below. On some damnably specific part of that earth, occupying her life to the very edges of the frame, Janelle was no doubt laughing with the jingling, sexual sound of all that new cash in her voice. Perhaps (now squinting to look through the cold-frosted porthole) she was recounting to friends the story of the moron who, in an access of startling credulity, had collaborated in the extraction of nearly his entire net worth.

He stared balefully out the window. Two days earlier he had driven to see the PI whom Bortz had recommended. Bortz had described him as a "somewhat peculiar individual" who happened to be the best "skip tracer" on the planet, and "supremely gifted" at finding missing persons. Potash, ringing the buzzer of an office that appeared to be merely the wing of a condo, was met by large man in his early fifties with a soft, somewhat disorganized face. Teddy Wilbraham wore a dark dressing gown and stood at the apex of a triangle of several small fox terriers that rushed forward and, as if in denial of their tininess, barked furiously at his feet.

"Welcome," he'd said in a deep, tired voice, holding out a hand.

One of the dogs snarled angrily at Potash and, bug-eyed, advanced forward on twig legs, trembling.

"Quite the fierce creature you've got there," Potash said, reaching out his hand to shake and smiling uncertainly.

"A stone-cold killer," said Wilbraham drily. "Please come in."

Nodding, Potash had stepped into the vestibule. It was a high-ceilinged space whose expensive terra-cotta floors and crown moldings hosted a scene of deep, apparently long-term disorder. Jackets hung higgledy-piggledy on pegs. Shoes were scattered around the floor. An aviary of scarves was tossed and wilting on hooks, and something ripe in the air made Potash want to breathe as shallowly as possible.

"Maid's day off," said Wilbraham, watching as Potash's eyes swiveled quickly around the space. "Would you like a coffee, Mr. . . . ."

"Potash. No thanks."

"Of course, like the mineral, sorry. Ach, my head," he said, turning and leading Potash down a long hallway while continuing to talk. "A night of indulgence, I'm afraid. The middle-aged hangover is a terrible thing to behold no doubt, but far worse to host. Please sit down"—he tapped a sofa—"and make yourself at home while I get that coffee for myself."

"Great, thanks."

Left alone, Potash noted that the waiting room continued the same theme of addled unkempt luxury. The expensive leather sofa on which he was seated had clearly seen better days, the signed Dali lithograph was askew, and the gryphon feet of a Regency armoire had been chewed by dogs. He identified the faint smell in the air as urine.

From a distant room, he heard Wilbraham shout, "I read your file. So sorry to hear of your recent troubles!"

"Thank you," Potash shouted back.

"Fraud"—there was a rattle of dishes—"is one of the boom sectors in an economic contraction, alas."

"Stands to reason," said Potash.

"They're linked like Laurel and Hardy all the way from the beginning of the modern market economy, you know. I was an adjunct professor at Fern Hills Community last year, in the economics department. Strangest thing, a little bit of education. Makes you realize how little things change over the years." There was the chortle of a coffeemaker, followed by the gargling sound of milk being steamed. "Oh, the terms change, along with the hairstyles, the clothes and all that sort of cultural thing, but the idea"—there was a pause of a few seconds, and then he strode out of the kitchen with a steaming coffee in hand—"of getting something for nothing seems part of human nature, I'm afraid."

"I'm not sure," Potash said slowly, "whether to be cheered or depressed by the thought that I belong to a tradition of fools."

"Well," said Wilbraham, sitting down, "membership does have its privileges."

"What?"

The investigator's large, soft face was creased by a sudden smile, giving Potash time to notice that his two front teeth were crossed one over the other like the legs of a sitting woman.

"A joke, Mr. Potash."

"Of course."

"To lighten your load."

"Got it," said Potash, as a dog barreled across the floor, snapped its head upward, launched its Thermos-sized body through the air, and landed square on Wilbraham's lap.

"Well, hello!" he cried, putting down his coffee and scratching the creature under the chin while it cocked its head and gazed gloatingly at Potash. "Yes," Wilbraham went on, "the people who battened on you are good, but then so are we." He turned to the dog. "Aren't we, Fenwick?"

He lifted his eyes abruptly to Potash. "Might I give you a word of advice?"

"Of course."

"Keep breathing. I noticed you stopped a few minutes ago."

The plane dove downward through shawls of cloud. With a bison rumble, the landing gear extended. Not long after, the satisfying shudder of the wheels touching earth announced their safe arrival at Kennedy. Potash, eyes shut, was watching Wilbraham airily request a five-thousand-dollar retainer, and he was watching himself sign over a check for half his remaining assets.

You didn't notice it until it was gone, indeed.

Deplaning, he strolled through the echoing concourse and then caught a cab, which rocketed toward Manhattan. From there, a bus took him north, into Connecticut, and twelve hours after having left his front door in California, Potash was standing at the still point of the turning world: the town he'd grown up in. Not far off was the large memory-museum of his home where his mother still lived, winding down like a dying satellite, her circuits to the store and nearby friends growing shorter, less frequent, more steeply angled each year.

A light rain had sprung up; he didn't mind. He began walking to his mother's house through the late-summer dusk, strolling up the long hill whose steepness as a child had been like a teacher instructing him in the outlines of his own will: if you're tired, walk slower; if you're stronger, walk faster; if you want to make something of yourself, run like the wind. He decided on a conservative middle-aged pace, and he soon arrived and rang the bell. A slow, sustained shuffling followed and then the door swung wide, and his mother, wearing a shapeless housedress and her short fitted cap of gray hair, leaned forward out the door, smiled at him with unnaturally square false teeth and cried, "Well, hello! You got rained on, eh?"

"Yup," he reached forward, but she held him an extra second by the elbows, wanting to get an opening shot in. "And you look like a drowned rat."

"Lovely to see you too," he said.

She laughed and hugged him. Quick, cutting exchanges were her specialty, and the way—he'd learned long ago—she protected her nearly crippling tenderness.

"So, come in."

He entered the house, following her down the hallway whose details he knew as well as the moles and hair patterns of his own body: the plaster sculpture of an archer, poised forever to strike; the "Greek" etching of women with lutes; the grand piano crouched like a partly open sarcophagus. His parents had been defiantly "European" and classical in their inclinations, even as, inexplicably, they fetched up in this bedroom community of New York, among bluff, foursquare middle Americans who knew little about their interests and cared less. His father was a failed historian of science turned businessman; his mother was a failed ballet dancer turned piano teacher. In the space behind those failures lay a profound appreciation for the old world, and in distinction to the bright, cheerful, utterly contemporary home lives of his friends, Potash had grown up with parents whose axial lines rode back into the darkening sepia tones of the past.

A lot of good that had done him.

"Have you heard from Robert lately?" he asked.

Robert was his four years younger, doted-on, can-do-no-wrong sibling, who had finally stepped forward, at Potash's request, and undertaken the heavy lifting of actually remaining in his mother's orbit, and of providing the close-wired support she needed, when Potash had spun out west.

"Well, of course," she said, and he wondered if that was tartness in her voice. "He was out here just three days ago, in the station wagon, with a new set of patio furniture."

"Oh, good."

"Yes," she said slowly, staring at him with a strangely neutral or even disapproving look. "It was good."

He forgave her on the spot for playing him off his sibling. These psychic feints and dodges were as familiar to him as anything he knew, and it was fitting that, according to historical script, they would be taking place in the emotional epicenter of the home: the kitchen.

Potash tugged a squealing chair out from the table and sat down.

"You're keeping the place tidy," he said.

Rather than answer, she turned away from him toward the stove.

He saw the slumped shoulders, the slow, gathering contractions of old age, and felt a childlike pang of sympathy for his mother.

"Not me, but Alvester," she said, mentioning the longtime maid.

A few moments of silence passed, and then she stopped what she was doing and turned to him. "John," she said simply, "did something happen? You look, I don't know what."

A sweet, sick feeling came over him. He recalled that he had first received his allowance in this very room. It was an elaborate ceremony conducted at this same plain pine kitchen table in which his father, with a great show of parsimony, individually counted out the shining coins into his hand. His father's brow, nose, the crooking vein on the forehead—the ever-fresh vividness of his own recollection astonished him.

"Ah, nothing much."

"I don't believe it."

"Let's talk about it later."

"You look tired, and I know from tired. The world too much with you?" she asked, intentionally mangling the Wordsworthian phrase.

"Sorta."

"Here." She had turned away from him a moment toward the oven, and now turned back with a fruit pie, still steaming. The oven door as she closed it made a particular squeal that he swore was among the oldest sounds he'd ever heard. He still remembered leaving Manhattan permanently for Connecticut. He was four years old, and it had been raining that afternoon—a warm summer rain—and the way the green of the lawns across the street ran in streaks and blobs on the rained-on windowpane was forever mixed up with his recollection of that day.

"For later," she said, "but smell." Swaddled in cloth, she put the oven dish under his nose a moment. Beneath the bubbling flour crust, a steam of sweet apples arose.

"Fantastic," he said, and meant it.

"Oh, please."

It was part of her program to rebuff his affection while mutely soliciting it in every way possible. Thereby working both sides of the street. She'd known he was coming, so in her eighties, hobbled by phlebitis, she'd dragged herself to the store in her ancient turret-shaped car and bought the wine he loved, and the treats. She put a bowl of pistachios on the table. From a nearby cabinet, moving with large, shaky dignity, she withdrew a bottle of red wine.

"Here. Sounds like you need it."

He opened the wine, poured, drank a large glass quickly. On an empty stomach, the alcohol went immediately to his head.

Potash breathed a long sigh of relief, as of a pressure being eased.

"They're unveiling Dad's stone the day after tomorrow," she said.

"Yes, Mom, I know," he said, not wanting to remind her faltering memory that he was here for precisely that reason.

"And I got the phrase on it I wanted."

"What one?"

"*Per aspera ad astra.*"

"Which means?"

"Through difficulties to the stars."

For a moment, overcome, he could not speak. His father had been an amateur historian of celestial navigation, and Potash had spent much of his childhood alongside his father sweeping backyard telescopes through the pinpoint infinities of nighttime skies. After his father's death, experimentally, he had taken the telescope out into the backyard again in the fanciful attempt to see if by some chance . . . there was actually some bright new celestial body shining in the heavens. The gesture was absurd, but then so was death in its remorseless refusal to negotiate its imperial discontinuity with the rest of life.

"Do you miss him?" his keen, intuitive old mother now asked.

"Terribly, yes."

"Me too," she said. A silence extended itself in the room. "And so," she said finally, mostly to herself, "it goes."

Potash, to keep his composure, had to look away.

CHAPTER SIXTEEN

Something either wondrous or horrible had happened, depending on your point of view. He had resisted at the last minute. Already in the bolting sexual flow of it, with her tongue in his mouth and the blood pounding in his body, something in him had retracted back, sharply, and with a kind of sorrowing regret, he'd said, "No, I don't think so." He'd gently pressed her away from him, stood up and said, "I'm just feeling this is all wrong and I can't do it, sorry."

"Really?" She was astonished. And in the wake of that he saw her composure crack; a kind of gashed look of surprise came over her, and she shook her head wonderingly. That wonder soon hardened into a look of contempt. She started to say something, thought the better of it. Then she stood up, shrugged her shoulders as if to say, Whatever, snatched up her computer, and while he watched, marched stiffly out of the room.

She left behind a furious kind of odor in the air, as of excited molecules and her perfume mixed, and he sat there for a moment, breathing this in while he collected his thoughts. What had just happened to him, he believed, had been a test of a sort, sent winging into his life from the far reaches of the universe. And in response, after some initial slippage, he'd done the right thing. But there was something else there as well. Because this girl was a player, or a "polyhedral" as he sometimes privately called such types of people in recognition of their many-sidedness (or fraudulence), she had an ulterior motive of some sort. That being the case, what did she want?

Whatever it was, the important point, he thought, getting to his feet, his blood subsiding, was that he'd unmistakably dodged a bullet with this chick; or more than a bullet, a train full of fury and light that had just blown by an inch away from his face and left his hair still hanging sideways in the breeze.

As best he could, he washed the traces of her off himself in the cramped office bathroom and drove home with the sense of the ordinary daily operations of his life haloed with a light of reprieve.

The front of his house, as he pulled up—how peaceful it looked! And the small breast of lawn, as he got out and stood on it—how easily he could have lain down and fallen asleep on it! The positive *thunk* of the front door seemed to signal a final separation from himself and the kingdom of the mad. And the air of the house, the very atoms of it, were deeply, reassuringly familiar.

"Glyn?" His voice went out tentatively.

"Oh, hi!" His wife turned a corner and stood smiling at him from five feet way. "You look tired, honey."

"Do I? Nothing a drink wouldn't cure."

Spectacularly, incredibly, she did nothing at all aside from saying, "I think we can accommodate that. Give me a few minutes to finish something up first, and then let's go sit in the garden, okay?" And with that, and a wink, she turned around and went into the kitchen.

And Lawrence walked very carefully to his study, then plopped down in his easy chair and felt an iceberg of remorse calving gracefully off his body and landing with a splash hundreds of feet below.

Over the next few days, he found himself unnaturally cautious about the operations of his own life. Already organized by nature, he became obsessively so. He was on a break between seminars of a few weeks, and he drew up an exhaustive schedule of home improvement tasks and decided to advance some of the periodic maintenance as well. He didn't want to think. He wanted to busy himself in small jobs dedicated to improving the state of his home, and by extension, his marriage. By passing his waking hours patching, painting, stripping, caulking, and at night, plotting the next day's work in his Day-Timer, he allowed himself as little as possible time for introspection, and he found this arrangement agreeing with him.

One evening around this time, his wife and he were having dinner in the garden. As luck would have it, Glynis had made one of his favorite seasonal meals: steamed haricots verts from the garden, along with spring lamb, broiled with rosemary and garlic, accompanied by a big round Italian red. They were seated at the small round table in the garden, amid a bower of the flowering plants and vines that it had been her pride to cultivate.

Very casually, she said, "So I was thinking of something."

"Really?" He looked up at her with his fork poised. "What was that, honey?"

"Randolph Crisp," she said.

"Oh, really? Why?"

Randolph Crisp was a man they'd both heard of through mutual friends who was the founder of something called Sexual

Yoga. A cult figure of a sort, he toured the country doing workshops in an arrangement not entirely dissimilar to those of Lawrence's: a hundred or two hundred or so people in a room together for a weekend. The subject of his work was the polarity between a man and a woman, and his workshops promised "renewed emotional attachment, deepened ability to love, and the rekindling of sexual sparks."

"Oh, you know." She looked at him, blushing, and he noticed that she'd put on lipstick—she had Cupid's bow lips.

"I'm touched," he was smiling, "that you're thinking like that, honey. But it can get a little wild, can't it?"

"Maybe, but a woman in my book group was talking about it, and she said it was 'rejuvenating.'"

"Is that what you talk about in those groups?"

Her blush was deepening. On top of that, certain muscles around her mouth were now activating. This was the signal, in the face he knew better than any other in the world, that she was playfully overriding her own reservations about something for the sake of the greater good of their togetherness. Love, experienced as heat, widened in his chest.

"Don't you think?" she asked.

"Yes," he said, "I do."

He made the reservations later that night. A day and a half later, bags packed, they were threading their car deep into New York State up Route 17, and then, after two hours, pulling off the main highway and entering a series of secondary roads. Around a turn they suddenly noticed a large compound with panoramic views set high on a nearby hill. The curving driveway led past a sign that said LEAVE YOUR VICES HERE, with an arrow indicating a nearby trash can. The place as they entered it had the air of a highly structured summer camp. There was an outdoor registration desk and about a hundred or so people were strolling the enormous lawns. Many of them walked hand in hand. Lawrence and Glynis signed in, unpacked in their upstairs room in the giant rambling mansion and watched out their window as Crisp arrived in a van. Aside from some blurry clandestinely shot YouTube videos, Crisp had rarely been seen by anyone, except at his seminars. The van first debouched at least six beautiful female attendants wearing identical sweatpants and skimpy white T-shirts before Crisp followed them. He was thin, with long center-parted hair, chinos and an unnaturally erect posture. He acknowledged no one and was hustled immediately indoors and out of sight.

"The guru doth underwhelm," said Glynis, who was standing alongside him at the window. They both laughed.

Later that afternoon, after a vegetarian lunch served in a wood-paneled dining hall, they all convened in a kind of large home theater, which a hand-lettered sign indicated was the KIVA. The attendees were segregated by sex and grouped sitting on the carpeted floor in a rough semicircle around a small elevated stage. Crisp strode onto this stage and stood before them, smiling, now dressed in brown cargo pants, a chambray shirt, and sandals over wool socks. His hair was gathered in a ponytail.

"We're here today to talk about sex, death and love," he said. "Any questions?"

Everyone laughed, Lawrence included. When silence fell, Crisp looked out at them and slowly swept his gaze from side to side before beginning to speak in his real voice, which was soft and hypnotic.

"What you once loved as a child has already been forgotten by you. And that which you love now even passionately will eventually dwindle and disappear. The bulb of the flower already contains within it the precise directions for that flower's death. But eternity is knowable in the here and now, my friends. That eternity is found in understanding your deepest purpose. It consists in giving the world the gift you were born to give. And in traveling through the cosmic portal of sex into the heart of that thing which makes us crucially human: love."

Without looking at her, Lawrence knew that his wife was sitting primly across the room, staring outward with that expression on her face of somewhat sad containment which she often adopted in public. He felt closer to her at that moment, separated and in an alien setting, than he could remember feeling in a long time.

"Women," Randolph said, surveying the female side of the room, "we adore and worship you. We understand that when you're relaxed in your heart, you are the apex of God's creation, filled to the brim with life and as wide and open, as changeable and deep, as the ocean."

"Men," he said, turning to the other side of the room and making a face of obvious distaste, "you're a disappointment. When faced with the oceanic beauty of women, you usually attempt to turn it into a swimming pool. You wall it off, cheapen it whenever possible, and try to make of it something you can control and cross with the boat of your will."

He turned back to the center. Light on his feet, he swayed in one direction and then another before raising a hand straight in the air and lowering it until it was pointing directly in front of him like a rifle.

"You," he said.

The man sitting next to Lawrence stiffened.

"Me?"

"Yes, you. Could you come up here, please?"

The man got to his feet. Balding and thin, wearing khakis and a black T-shirt, he sported a trim pencil mustache.

"What's your name?" Randolph asked him as he made his way onto the stage.

"Clarence."

"Clarence," Randolph said, "is trying to appeal to women by showing us through the mustache on his face just how virile he can be. Well, Clarence, here's your chance. I want you right now to put on your sexiest face, the one you give to a woman who you want to seduce, and I want you to give us your best bedroom line.

"Ladies," he went on as he turned away from the now-frowning Clarence to the women's side of the room, "I want you to respond by making the sound that his approach elicits in you."

Clarence's frown deepened. He looked physically ill for a moment before lowering his head to prepare himself. A moment later he flung it back up while putting his hands on his hips and thrusting his chest out. He drew his lips into the rictus of a man trying to initiate a particularly stubborn bowel movement.

"Hello, baby," he said, "can I draw you a hot bath?"

A high, long, derisive groan met this line. The women hooted at the now-crimsoning Clarence. He stopped. He seemed to shrink onstage.

"How would you describe the size of your penis about now?" asked Randolph to an eruption of laughter.

"See," said Randolph, as Clarence slunk back to his spot next to Lawrence, "this is exactly what I'm talking about. Men have no idea what women want, and our Clarence was basically spouting lines he'd seen on a television show or in some silly self-help book. He was doing what men do best: follow the script rather than walk through life with their eyes open. When a man stands in his power, the woman is attracted. It's a law of nature, like gravity or entropy. But when a man merely mouths empty platitudes at a woman while he waits for her to take his clothes off, then that man is doomed to failure."

Lawrence noted how, differently from himself, Randolph was an orator, a person adept at producing rhetorical effects and placing his audience in a kind of trance. Studying him more carefully, he observed that despite the apparent warmth, Randolph had unnaturally straight lower eyelids, indicating that he privileged logic over feeling, and the rounded, bulbous nose of a pleasure-seeker.

Pleasure—of the carnal variety—was the order of the day's discussion, and that night, in their room, Lawrence and Glynis fell upon each other with the kind of unfettered passion that had been missing from their marriage for years. After they were done, while lying in bed, through the thin walls of the house they heard the unmistakable sounds of others carrying on similarly.

The next day, the exercises began. The couples were split up and the partners reassigned. Each of them was then asked to flirt with his or her new partner as both a man and a woman. Lawrence found this well outside his comfort zone, but good-naturedly tried to comply, batting his eyes in a grotesque parody of female wiles and jutting his hips. He also tried to comply when he and Glynis were reunited and sat with their eyes shut, knees touching and fingers lightly resting on each other's hands as they drew collaborative shapes in the air with these hands at Randolph's command. This apparently innocent exercise contained a wicked undertow. As it went on, Lawrence found the entire emotional curvature of their marriage replicated in miniature in the dance of their fingers: he needing to save her and she responding with ambivalence at this gallantry; she refusing to catch him when he fell, and he, despite his avowed self-sufficiency, feeling abandonment at those moments. This apparently innocent series of micromovements eventually enraged both of them.

As the day drew on, Lawrence began quite clearly to see the bigger picture, and the deeper outlook behind Randolph's apparently eccentric exercises. Simply, by putting one's sexuality on the line, one regenerated some of that sexuality, and regenerated as well the polarity between a man and a woman that was crossed in sex.

"What a strange, smart man he is," said Glynis, at lunch.

Again, that night, following an afternoon of "fire-breathing" exercises designed to simulate orgasm, he found himself making love to his wife for hours.

The next morning Randolph met the attendees at breakfast and mingled. A celebratory ease was in the air. This small encampment two hours north of Manhattan had hosted a twenty-four-hour marathon of riotous sex, and it showed in the calmly unprotected way everyone spoke with one another and the expanded feeling of bonhomie in the air. Lawrence stared at his wife across the table as she ate lunch with a newly fresh shyness to her motions that was her inherent modesty and was particularly striking after her sexual abandon of the night before. He adored her for it. He adored her strength equally as much as he loved her gentle reserve.

They bid good-bye, and on the two-hour drive back he found himself returned to a chatty, flirtatious warmth with his wife that felt like a restoration of some primary and long-gone sentiment. He'd forgotten how lovely she was as she smiled and allowed the thickening sound of desire back into her voice. The eros of their early years together had gradually become cluttered with the busy-work of life—and it wasn't until this weekend that he realized how much he'd missed it.

Neither of them had turned on their BlackBerrys since arriving at the retreat because they wanted to give the weekend a full chance to work its magic on them without distraction. But twenty-five minutes after having left the compound, having flicked them on in the meantime, they were rounding a seemingly endless turn around a large forested mountain and laughing hard about a comic mishap involving a ne'er-do-well cousin of hers when the crisp electronic beeps sounded out of the machines, reestablishing contact. Lawrence watched as she picked his up with a glancing laughing look in her eye, as if daring him to interrupt her. The sunshine flared against the screen and effectively rendered it opaque. She twisted it a moment in her hands, and the writing became visible. Stacked in the middle of the page were four identically titled e-mails to him. Even though he was proceeding around a large curve in the road at that moment, he saw them clearly.

In capital letters glowing blackly on the screen were written repeatedly the words *I BURN 4 U*, leading like a small, inevitable staircase down the page.

CHAPTER SEVENTEEN

Men spoke a stench, and none more so than her pious, sentimental fraud of a dad. After he died—lingeringly, horribly—she moved, with great relief, to New York. She was done with Northampton, with eking out a living padded with the occasional theft of her family's funds; with seething at her friends whose cards and letters continued somewhat tauntingly to float into her mailbox. She'd had it with that sense of slowing orbits and deepening boredom relieved only by the stray overcompensating numskull wandering into her bed.

Through friends, she procured an internship at a small up-and-coming fashion magazine named Cachet. She bunked with some acquaintances on the Lower East Side and entered the mouth of the subway each morning at a shabby intersection and exited it twenty minutes later like Venus on the half shell into a zone of affluence and pretension. The magazine was housed in a landmark building on the Upper East Side and was known for its outlandish mix of street and couture. It was there that she met Lulu Bach.

Lulu Bach, her boss and the editor in chief of the magazine, was a tall, physically powerful woman whose face wore the perpetually wide-

awake stencil of plastic surgery. Swathed most often in clingy black couture—Marc Jacobs, Prada, or her old friend Michael Kors—she was quick-witted and foghorn-loud and appeared to savor her own falsity. The phonier she was, the more everyone liked it. It was the first time Margot saw how badly irony beat candor in New York; she would never forget the lesson.

"Good morning!" That familiar, cheery voice again. She opened her eyes. Dan France the unshakable was there, giving his openhearted smile. He reminded her of certain rock formations. He reminded her of large midwestern corporations with conservative bottom lines. He was insistent on hanging around with the same old buzz in his pants and itchy fingers, while pretending to live exclusively among higher, drier, purer things. Men! She smiled at him, prettily. At least he was hand-some. She was feeling better and better each day.

"Good morning, sharpshooter," she said.

"I've got news for you," he said.

"What's that?"

"You're getting out of here."

"Really? Where?"

"To rehab. You're ready for the big time now."

She studied him, carefully.

"When?" she asked.

"Some time in the next few days. The facility is nearby. You'll still have restricted movement, of course, and will be on meds, but you can get out of this white box and into a place with a bit more life in it. You like?"

He was nearly panting with excitement.

"Um," she said.

She was remembering how she fetched Lulu's coffee every morning; brought her pastries and memos, ran errands, sat mostly silent at the weekly staff meetings, and observed the daily operations of her world. Lulu had nicknames for everyone and quickly dubbed her Smith in deference to her college, and in that honking loud voice that Lulu seemed to relish for how strikingly it was out of keeping with the rest of her white-powdered cloisonné features, she would shout, "Where's my damn Smith!"

"I was cleared to take you out to lunch today," Dan France said. "Would you like that?"

"Sure," she said. "I'll ring for the nurse to help me change. Can you, uh, like, disappear for five minutes?"

"But of course." He nearly giggled as he scampered out of the room.

Every three months or so, Lulu would have a party at her loft on Mercer Street and select staff would be invited. The high, square space, with coffered tin ceilings, pickled wooden floors and dark walls, had been converted by Lulu into a seashell temple. Armed with a glue gun she had stickered every wall with cockles, razor clam shells, tiny cowries and scallop shells. Amid this stranded sampler of marine life, waiters in half tuxes circulated carrying tiny silver trays, while Lulu moved like a huntress of high spirits, her voice expansive, pitched to impress.

"This is Smith," she cried to magazine editors, artists, costume designers and the many junior executives in bespoke suits and millimetrically bias-cut hair who were flattered to be out among the "creatives" for a night. "This is Smith and if you don't watch it, she'll have your job lickety-split!" she cried. "She seems demure," she bellowed over the portobello spears, the fried guanciale rolls, and the Kobe carpaccio, "and dammit, she is demure, that's the thing. But she's also a tiger, guaranteed!"

"Are you really a tiger?" a man asked her, coming up behind her, and smiling into her face.

She was learning to take the measure of people quickly, on the fly. She'd arrived in New York with a receptive openness that hovered in the dangerous interspace between ingenue and bumpkin. The challenge, she understood, was to judge while not seeming to, like doing the crossword while jogging in place.

"Meow," she said to the man, "have I seen you before?"

He had the kind of face she liked, where the prettiness was marred or emphasized by a single outsize feature, in this case his nose. He had long, light-colored lashes, like a giraffe. He was tall and about thirty-five.

He bowed at the waist. "If you haven't," he said, "then I sincerely apologize."

The nurse was helping her dress in a white shirt and loose pants. She was moving slowly, because every time she moved quickly, she felt that something might spill. There were names for this condition. She took drugs for this condition. It was a slow road back from a brain injury as serious as the one she'd received. She was placed, with the nurse's aid, in a wheelchair.

Dan France was waiting in the hall. He looked bashful and excited. "Thanks, ma'am," he said to the nurse, smoothly cutting in and taking the handles of the wheelchair. He pushed her gently down the long corridor while she inhaled the unpleasant smell of the hospital: organic rot barely masked by pine.

"I've decided to look more into your background," said Dan France, fifteen minutes later, when they were seated at a local restaurant. The wheelchair, at its lowest setting, had been slid under the table.

"Oh?" She felt a reflex twinge.

"Yes, because I've been told the occasional thing about you from other people in the department, and I want to make sure everything is shipshape and watertight."

"What kind of things have you been hearing?"

"Just things," he said.

The restaurant seemed too large, too loud; the frame of space was off; it billowed. She suddenly wanted to be back in her hospital bed, but she looked down, gathered herself and repeated, "What kind of things?"

"Inconsistencies in the paper trail, and stuff like that. But let's not worry about it now. Documents have a way of sorting themselves out. What we want is to have you back on your pins, pronto. Everything else will take care of itself."

He laid his large open hands on the table in an inviting gesture and smiled. His eyes were resting level in hers. She was remembering, hard. Men could be rotated at will after sex, but it was before sex that the more crucial adjustments were always made.

She touched her hand to his and instantly, like a startled reef fish, it swerved and shut closed on her fingers. "To paraphrase a dead writer I admire," she said softly, "you have a certain syrup, Dan, and I like the way it pours."

CHAPTER EIGHTEEN

"Oh Christ, it must be that girl," Lawrence said, continuing to drive as his wife slowly placed the incriminating BlackBerry down on the seat and he gripped the steering wheel as if bracing himself against a sudden burst of wind.

"Girl," she said carefully.

"The one I was giving privates to. Jesus!" he said.

"Privates," she said.

"Yes, you remember, honey." Keeping his eyes on the road, he went to place his hand on her arm. But the arm was not there.

"Vaguely," she said. "And?"

"And nothing," he said. "She was a crazy girl who wanted something from me, and hounded me, and called and kept coming to privates and paying for them of course, and then one day, she tried to kind of push matters with me."

"Oh, really," his wife said to the windshield of the car.

"Yes," he said. "Problem was, I pushed back."

Out of the side of his eye, he watched her lips open and then her face turn down.

"She thrust herself on me, honey. I mean aggressively."

"Uh-huh." Her voice was dangerously soft.

"Darling?" He swiveled his eyes toward hers in time to see her *corrugators supercilii* muscles firing in the classical eyebrow contraction of grief, and he felt a sudden murderous gust of rage toward the girl, Margot.

"What I'm about to tell you is the utter truth," he went on calmly, "and I will say it as many times as you need to hear it. This person attacked me physically, making advances during one of our private lessons, and, yes, I kissed her briefly back but then I pushed her away. The rejection seems to have made her nuts and driven her into some kind of revenge strategy where she's pretending we're actually an item. I don't think she's used to being rejected is my hunch, and so she's lying to try to damage me. And that's it."

But instead of saying anything, all she did was look down into her lap, swallowing audibly several times.

"Honey!" he said, touching her trembling back while squelching the desire to shout, *I was preyed upon, dammit! I was ambushed by a miserable creature who used the traction of a single kiss to try to wound both of us! That's the truth!*

Instead, in an uncertain voice, he asked, "Glynis?"

When she said nothing, he went on in a low voice, "Agreed that I should have told you. But it seemed so very little, at bottom. I mean, really."

There was a long silence.

"Did you sleep with her?" she asked suddenly, swiveling her head around on her neck and intercepting his glance with an impact that traveled down from his eyes to his hands like a twitch along a length of rope. The car veered to the left.

"Of course not!" He brought the car back to center.

She returned to looking straight ahead, giving him absolutely no sign that she'd heard. The car purred along the interstate. He fiddled uselessly with the controls of the AC. Twice over their marriage of eighteen years he had slipped and fallen all the way down the long, tumbling chute of lust into the bed of a young female student. Both times he had terminated the affair within a week, tearfully telling all to his wife, and both times she'd left not long after, taking an extended vacation with a girlfriend devoted to "reconsidering" their marriage. While she was away, Lawrence, determined to find the bright side of his infidelity, had told himself these dalliances were "contrast gainers" of a sort, which allowed him, from the far side of the chaos and pain they'd engendered, a new appreciation of the calm, deep-water harbor of his marriage. In the aftermath of this perception, he threw himself into reconciliation with renewed ardor. And Glynis, who invariably returned from her trips puffy-faced beneath her tan and with a sad, high-hearted desire to separate, both times let herself be swayed by his contrition.

Outwardly impassive, he continued heatedly to argue his case to himself as they drove. By the time they were nearing home, nearly an hour had drifted by in perfect silence. They were turning into their home street when a violent gust of hatred of Margot again tore through his heart. But that was crazy too, said a wiser, older voice in his head. His wife was understandably gun-shy, even though this had been merely a kiss, and what was needed now was the grace of pardon—of himself, mainly, but of her as well.

Gently, he touched her shoulder, as they moved toward the door down the winding flagstone path. Hadn't his prior delinquencies—because he thought of them that way, as youthful indiscretions like cutting school or stealing cars—eventually been reabsorbed into the larger mass of their married happiness? Of course they had.

Time was absorptive; it had always handily blotted up difficulties in the past. Somewhere in the not too distant future, holding hands, perhaps, and on vacation in one of those mountain towns he loved in the American West or Europe where the sheer immensity of space acted to shrink the human drama to bearable dimensions, they'd be seated on a little wooden bench in a fieldstone inn, toddies in hand, and would revisit this moment, and laugh their heads off, with the rueful, easy laughter that accrues exclusively to partners in long-term marriages.

Then he opened the door.

CHAPTER NINETEEN

The next morning, despite having slept terribly that night in his childhood bed, Potash was a guilty whirlwind. He raked the leaves out of his mother's backyard drainage ditches; cleaned the oil off the garage floor where it had dripped from her ancient car. He inspected the rubber moldings of her windows, tightened the bolts on the banisters, mucked out the dishwasher, and in general, he believed, gave a good accounting of himself as a concerned, responsible firstborn son sprucing up and looking after his elderly mother.

With one terrible exception.

"So what happened, John?" she asked him that evening, landing on the very question he somehow thought his industry, his filial loyalty, his essential goodness would override. He was seated at the kitchen table while he watched her come toward him bearing a steaming tureen of soup, before sitting down in front of him, slowly, with the sense of moving many different parts into a kind of rough collaboration, and then staring at him, heavy-lidded.

"What do you mean?" he asked.

"The same thing as when I asked you yesterday. You don't seem yourself, is what. You wanna talk?"

"Well, Mom," he said softly, deciding that a little bit of the truth, eyedroppered homeopathically into their conversation, couldn't hurt, "I did have a little bit of a financial, uh, reversal."

She began shaking her head slowly side to side. "Oof," she said, "that's terrible. And especially now. Bad investment?"

"Essentially, yes."

"Does Anabella know?"

He smiled at her priorities. His mother was secretly convinced, he sometimes felt, that he didn't deserve a woman as beautiful and openhearted as his new wife. She seemed perpetually in fear that Anabella would somehow discover the truth about him and show him the door.

"No, she doesn't."

"Well, that's good. "

Potash stared silently into his lap, and then some surge of self-revulsion, some desire to make a clean breast of it, caused him to say, "But I lost a lot."

"Really?" Her eyes sharpened. "And you can't get it back?"

"Probably not, though I'm trying."

"Well, so how much?" she asked, and that original strange tremor of self-revulsion, deepening rapidly, snatched the words out of his mouth.

"Most of my savings, along with a big chunk of Anabella's too."

She brought a hand to her lips and gave a weak, high little cry.

"No, God! And our nest egg?"

He nodded, miserable, while she slumped in her chair and became visibly smaller. Once, watching a rogue elephant shot on a game preserve, he'd seen how the impact of its death, in waves, finally reached the thoughtful old creature. Its initial response had been to grow older on the spot. His mother grew older.

"It's impossible," she said, reaching forward and loading a huge slab of butter onto her corn muffin.

"Mom, your cholesterol."

"The hell with my cholesterol!"

She would at least loan him her disgust. She had emotions enough for the two of them, and refinement and profanity were the flip sides of her temperament.

"Goddamnit to hell!" she shouted in her raspy high voice.

Potash reached out to touch her reassuringly, but then he interrupted the gesture halfway and drew back his hand. "I know," he said. "I feel like a complete idiot. No, that's not what I feel. I feel . . . oh, who cares what I feel."

"It's a signal," she was muttering to herself. "It's a signal it's all over. Otherwise, why? It makes no sense. Always something, and if not this, then that, and if not that, then the other, with no end in sight, ever." She shut her eyes and began singing in a low voice, "Oh no, honey, tell me about the money, tell me about the money in the here and now." Then she opened her eyes again. "Maybe I misheard. Say it again, but this time with a happy ending. Tell me it's not true, John."

"I wish it wasn't so, Ma. But yes, it is."

"Is it a woman thing?" she asked suddenly.

"What?"

She continued staring at him. "You heard me."

"What are you talking about?"

By degrees, the natural warmth was leaving her face. A harsh, stony look was coming over her. "You're a smart boy, and smart boys don't usually lose everything unless they turn dumb, or a little birdie makes them that way."

"Please."

She cupped a hand to her large ear. "I didn't hear you deny it."

"Okay. I deny it."

"How nice for you. You think I'm stupid?"

No, he did not. She'd never been anyone's dupe. She'd married a man she loved and dutifully stood by his side as they marched in old-fashioned lockstep through a world whose shocks and distortions they could never have foreseen. And now that she was at the end of the line, she wanted, justifiably, to have some peace.

Instead, he'd come creeping around with his wheedling needs, his heartstring-tickling bullshit. And furthermore, astonishingly, she was right. It *was* a sex thing, in the broadest terms.

Potash looked away from her, to the bow windows where the great-great-grandchildren of the same birds that had accompanied his earliest boyhood memories skipped and fussed in the branches, tweeting with the same brainless, ever-fresh gusto as ever.

"And the police?" she asked.

"Nothing there," he said to the window, grateful for a conversational avenue leading away from himself. "I made calls, but the police quickly passed me to people at the FBI. The word I got back is that, yes, they can send their fraud units into action and build a case, but the chances of recovery of my, uh, assets, are, in the words of the articles I've read, 'disappointingly small.' However, I've hired a private investigator."

He looked into her face for consolation but saw nothing there.

"But you had lots of money, John."

"I know."

"I mean, lots of money, ours and your own. You were doing so very well."

There it was again: the square, settled certainty that had been part of the birthright of her generation. If you had something, you kept ahold of it: whether it was savings, a house or a spouse.

"Yes," he said.

Again a long sigh. He knew that one day he'd hear that same gravelly outflow of breath, with no intake following it, and she'd be gone, vanished with astonishing totality—the entire person down to the tiniest grains simply whisked away into the void. A week, a month from now, a year if he were lucky. The mystery of his human origins thereby sealed forever shut, and the directional wind of life picking up speed toward his own oblivion.

"Mom," he said softly.

On the plane ride over, he had briefly entertained the wild idea of asking her to do a reverse mortgage on her house, thereby freeing up a few hundred thousand dollars for him and his brother to divide. This was grotesque and unseemly. It smelled bad in his own nose. But aloft in the suspended enclosure of the plane, it had briefly seemed reasonable.

"John," she said simply in response, and he saw the real, undeniable pain in her face, and his own heart misgave him for even thinking such a thing. He was looking for succor; he was hoping she might extend a protective canopy over his exposed head as she had so many times during his childhood and prevent the inclemencies of life from drumming him senseless. But to ask her to rescue him at her advanced age, and in his state of looming bankruptcy and confusion—it was beyond dishonorable. It was unthinkable.

On the spot, inventing clumsily, he said, "But the good news is that Anabella's brother has these ancient bonds, these old munis that he never cashed in, and he's giving us a bridge loan. I'm telling you all this now because, well, I needed to get it off my chest and clear my conscience, you know?"

"John," she repeated in the identical intonation, clearly disbelieving him, and then, saying nothing more, she began to eat. He smiled, feeling sick to his stomach, and ladled himself a bowl of soup and raised a spoonful to his mouth. It was astonishingly good.

CHAPTER TWENTY

The rehab center was like a hospital minus all the cold medical bits. The corridors were sunnier, the smells were gentler, the sounds were softer, and the rooms weren't filled with beaked and horrible machinery for removing parts of you. Instead, there were large, high-ceilinged spaces with mats on their floors as thick as puddings, along with piles of stretchy bright rubber bands that many of the elderly residents pulled with their knees and the dwindled chicken wings of their arms. There were shower chairs with too many armrests for putting you in and wheeling you into the shower if your legs didn't work; heat rooms, cold rooms, weight rooms and gym rooms; rooms with plunge baths, and rooms piled full of bolsters and foam wedges like gardens of geometrical clouds.

The problem was that the staff of the facility was so nice, and so eager to help, and looked at you with such emotions of sympathy and understanding, that it was all she could do not to drive a plastic fork into their eyes. It was coming back, oh yes it was, and one thing coming with it was the feeling that the worst people were frequently the nicest, and if that were the case, then she was among some of the very worst people on earth.

Twice a day, she was scheduled to do an hour or two of therapy. Her physical therapy was all about balance, and her therapist was a little bouncing ball of a man named Nino. Under his direction, she tried—and failed—to hop like a frog, or stand on one foot and attempted to raise her other leg until it was parallel to the floor. She walked wobbling in a circle wearing special ankle weights and a weighted vest while watching the city turn in the opposite direction outside the window, many floors below. In another series of lessons she spent time on memory and cognition, rowing her mind up and down sequences of numbers, filling in the blanks, reading out loud, or doing word associations.

Too often, in the downtime when she didn't have to do anything, and would have been happy merely to lie in bed with the past walking across her mind, Dan France was there. He was there a lot. He wore casual clothes and a permanent smile, like a plaque. He looked at her with a melting look that was clearly his idea of what cute was. He was used to being admired. He was used to being listened to. At least he was handsome. But did he know how obvious he was?

Then, one day, he tried to kiss her. She saw it coming like a sailboat over the horizon line. She sat in a chair in her room while he put his hands on her shoulders and raised himself up on his toes and gave her his warmest smile and bent over at the waist to lean in close.

On the television above her bed, tuned to the closed-circuit view of the rehab underground parking garage, cars, like silverfish, darted regularly in and out of open spaces.

"What," she said.

She knew exactly what. The kiss would be the opener for the doggishly attentive Dan France, and a day, a week or a month afterward, he would clumsily fold his forepaws over her shoulders and then push his red, wet erection back and forth between her legs until it foamed over. He'd snarl and snap and bite her neck in his excitement and then lick her cheek when he was done.

"You," he said, doing abashed.

"What about me?"

"I'm digging you."

"Well, I'm feeling dug."

"How does that feel?"

"Better than a sock in the head."

"I think you're wonderful."

"Thanks," she said, stifling a tiny yawn.

"Margot?" He stood back up.

"Yup?" A speech, instead of a kiss. She hoped it wouldn't be a long one. Dan France was capable of floating lengthy air-deadeners at the drop of a hat.

"I thought," he said, "that it would be important that we get some stuff squared away." Now he squatted down in front of her. "'Cause you see," he said, "the gaps in the paper trail our people have collected on you are odd. I'm hoping they're not part of a deliberate pattern."

"Pattern?" Her eyes drifted back up to the TV set and the curvetting car-bugs. "How?"

Reaching behind him, he grabbed a chair one-handed and pulled it squealing toward him and sat down.

"Listen," he said, "is there anything you want to tell me?"

Her boredom was deepening.

"As in?" she asked.

"Anything," he said. "Anything at all?"

"I don't know. That I wish I was out of here? That the memory rehab stuff drives me nuts? That I wish I had been a fashion designer?"

"Fashion designer?"

"I always loved clothes."

"Well, what did you end up doing instead?"

"What?"

"What was the job you ended up doing in life, Margot?"

"You're the one with the answers, you tell me."

"Well, that's my point. Your paper trail is kinda unusual."

"So shoot me, Dan."

"No, I mean very unusual."

She looked at him directly, a measuring glance. "What are you trying to say?"

"Simply this." He leaned closer, and she was again struck by the sheer mass of him. "Our internal reporting people did a workup of you, following your Social Security records, your mailing addresses, your various driver's licenses and registration addresses and your tax returns. You seem to have had a fairly regular life as a college student and afterward. Paying your taxes, moving on up in life. At a certain point we have you going from Northampton to New York City. You get a job at a magazine called"—he looked down and riffled through his papers—"Cachet."

"Yes," she said, stifling the urge to yawn again, stronger this time. "That rings a bell."

"But here's the thing, Margot."

Her face was still held in the tension of a suppressed yawn when he said slowly, "After your stint at Cachet, you continue paying rent and utilities for your apartment, but for the rest, your paper trail, which is to say you, simply disappears into thin air."

CHAPTER TWENTY-ONE

The envelope lay on the floor like a clue. Rather than being placed in the mailbox at the foot of their driveway, it had been inserted by hand through the long-unused mail slot in the front door. Lawrence and Glynis stood at the entrance, luggage in hand.

"What is that?" she asked, speaking for the first time in an hour.

"Well, a letter obviously," he said, bending forward, picking up the envelope and turning it over in his hands. His name and address were neatly typed in the center, though no return address was given. Aware that she'd moved slightly closer and was looking over his shoulder, he pulled out the letter and then held it from the top, pinched in his fingers, as if to take as little possession of it as possible.

"What the hell?" he said slowly.

Dearest Lawrence, it read,

I know you're scared. I could tell you were frightened of the power of the feeling between us. It's why you acted as you did. I now understand everything. Please be patient with me, because I'm very vulnerable right now. But believe me when I say I can't wait to go to that place again.

Margot

The feeling for a moment was of falling through the words into a chasm of open space, before a guttural explosion of air behind his head caused him to spin around in time to see his wife literally running away from him into the house. "What?" he shouted, disbelieving. "Oh, come on, Glynis! You can't possibly think . . ."

But she was already stomping up the stairs, and after a moment of hesitation, he was running heavily after her, yanking himself upward with the help of the banister, while shouting, "Don't tell me you're falling for this, for God's sake! Please, honey, don't you see? Your reaction is exactly what she wanted. That's why she planted the letter there. Glynis!" But she put on a burst of speed, spun into the bedroom a few steps ahead of him, slammed the door shut, dead-bolted it with a heavy *thunk,* and then slammed the inner bathroom door shut as well. After a moment, audibly, she began running the shower.

He stood openmouthed with shock, serially pummeled by the uproars of first the scene in the car, and then this. As if, he thought, the girl was directing his afternoon on a large video screen in a war room, and pulling the various triggers perfectly on time. What should he do now? Shatter the bedroom door, burst into the shower and plead his case amid the pelting water? He had half a mind to. But what would that accomplish? He'd apologized already and had done nothing wrong between that moment and now. No, the wrong had come into their life from outside it, courtesy of the girl, who he'd made the mistake of allowing a half square inch of purchase on his inner world.

He went slowly back down the stairs to the kitchen, slumped in a chair and put his hands over his eyes. From the first, he had seen the signs—of her crookedness, her disingenuousness—and *still* fallen into the trap she'd laid. Was it because he'd come to think of himself as invulnerable; was that it? Thousands of people had attended his lectures over the years; tens of thousands had read his books. Had the sound of his own voice in his head somehow crowded out clear reasonableness? He raised his eyes and looked out the window to where the copse of fruit trees—peach, pear, apple—trembled guilelessly in the breeze.

For a long time he sat there, thinking furiously with nothing clear resulting. When the upstairs bedroom door finally opened and shut, the sound was as loud as a gunshot. This was followed a moment later by the emphatic thumps of feet on the stairs. His wife turned the corner with a brisk stride, and, involuntarily, he got to his feet.

Glynis had made herself up painstakingly, drawn on an attractive sheath skirt, heels, and a top that flattered her ample curves. She looked beautiful and rejuvenated, and having made love to her five times in the previous forty-eight hours, he felt a visceral desire to kiss her. Instead, his glance lowering over her body, he was shocked to see her clasping the handle of a small rolling bag.

"I've decided," she said calmly, "to allow you to do what you need to do."

"What?" His voice sounded strange to him. "What do you mean?"

"I don't know whether this is about the child," she said, using a phrase that was shorthand for a crazy season of their life, about ten years earlier, when they'd decided to try to have children, she'd gotten pregnant, miscarried, and at the doctor's insistence, had had a hysterectomy, "or your own midlife crisis, or a return to your previous cheating bullshit, but I don't care. I'm done with worrying about it."

"Done? What?" He heard the rising tones of panic inside his head and felt them particularly in his nostrils, where a sharp salt sensation prickled.

"I'm going to Marley's for a good while, to think things over and allow you to work things out."

Marley was her lone single friend, a loud, overdressed woman who was perpetually on the hunt for a good man. Reflexively, from the first time they'd met, Lawrence had detested her.

"Oh, come on, honey! Really?"

"Yes," she said.

"But this is ridiculous," he said. "It's a setup, plain and simple, and you're falling for it. I mean, can't you see that? Tell me you're not really that naive."

She smiled from a million miles away. "Up to your old tricks, Lawrence? Enjoy your superiority. It should be a great comfort in your new life."

He shook his head and said slowly, "It's not about my superiority, Glynis. It's the fact that you're going to offer up our marriage to a deranged woman, and in the process give her exactly what she wants."

She looked at him with a sad smile. "What do *you* want, Lawrence? You brought this woman into our marriage, I didn't. Or was it all an accident and did you accidentally"—she paused on the word for emphasis—"find yourself with your tongue in her mouth and God knows what else?"

"I can't believe this." He looked out the window as if to gather support from the cloudless afternoon. "So now you're putting our future in jeopardy because I made out for a half minute with an emotionally disturbed student?"

"Was she emotionally disturbed before she met you, or afterward?"

"Oh, for God's sake, stop it, please."

"I thought I knew you, yes I did. If you'd asked me as recently as last night, I would have said I did. But now?" She gave a long, rolling shrug of the shoulders.

A spasm of rage gripped him for a moment, and then passed, leaving in its place a deep fatigue.

"Well, then I'll miss you," he said simply.

"No, you won't."

He held his hands up on either side of his head and said loudly, "I can't believe what's happening here."

"What's happening," she said rapidly, "is that you've made it perfectly obvious what your priorities are, and I'm giving you the chance to explore them in peace. That's what's happening."

"No, what's happening is you're obeying word for word the script someone else has written for you, someone who happens to wish the worst for both of us!"

She began to walk away, but paused at the door and turned. "Do have fun sorting out your erotic issues with your friend, Lawrence," she said. "Because I'm sure the two of you will have a helluva lot to talk about."

And with that, his wife, who he couldn't remember ever looking so poised, centered, and nearly annealed in confidence, walked straight out of the living room, got into her car and drove away.

And he was left as thunderstruck as if a loitering tornado had stuck an arm of wind sideways through a window and yanked him all the way to Kansas.

That night Lawrence slept in the basement on a small pull-out sofa. The feeling of being in a subterranean chamber was vaguely comforting. The small television at the foot of the bed flickered and droned on for hours without consequence, like a drunk at a bar. Two, maybe three hours of dreamless sleep were all he got, and he woke the next morning feeling he'd been physically assaulted.

Moving up the stairs slowly, he crept into the sunny kitchen like a thief. Dog-eared magazines were piled in a straw hamper in a corner; oven mitts hung in a cluster like so many phantom hands; jars of beans and pastas ran in sequential order from large to small on a shelf over the stove, and farming prints of nineteenth-century life enlivened the walls. The wholesomeness of the scene was like a last, lingering wifely rebuke.

Strong coffee began to bring him around and gave him a clearer perception of himself as a man grotesquely overpunished for small indiscretions. He knew that though he wasn't conventionally attractive, to certain women his reserved, professorial manner and low-key wit were irresistible. Being a person so conversant with inner worlds, it was impossible that he not understand the affinities he could occasionally ignite in women.

But this woman was dangerous and unbalanced and he'd have to somehow neutralize her before she could do any more damage. It was on his second cup of coffee, and feeling the trademark jittery rush of bad energy coming on, that he managed to piece together the elements of an idea. To disarm the girl, he would have to meet her. To meet her, he would have to use bait. How bracing it was to think clearly! He trudged upstairs to his study, seated himself at his computer, took a last swig of coffee and with the feeling of lighting a small fuse of dynamite, typed the following words.

Margot my dear: I've been away, and have only now received your communication. I'm intrigued, but we must act very discreetly from here on in. For the moment, what do you say to us meeting in the near future? We should have dinner together.

"And I'll be waiting," he muttered, "to tear your fucking head off." But having said these terrible things aloud, he didn't necessarily believe them. Instead, he finished the e-mail, hit the Send button, lay his head on the desk, and in the middle of a busy morning, fell asleep with his head on his forearms.

CHAPTER TWENTY-TWO

As expected, the viewing of the gravestone was a wrenching experience. In the middle of sunshine and thriving, luxuriant grass that seemed cruelly to underline the finality of the occasion, they briefly bowed together. His mother wept quietly; his brother, always the emotional one, also wept, a little too loudly to his taste. Potash cried silently, the tears dripping, stinging, the three of them loosely embracing, swaying slightly, each lost in his or her thoughts. If emotions could be bodied forth in images, then the moment of feeling would have been represented as a large glistening bubble of a sort grown like a dome over the spreading lawns where his father, that quester after the origins of stars, would now forever rest on earth.

Later that day, bags packed, he stood in the vestibule, heartsore but ready to return home at last. But his mother, now that the weekend was over, seemed indifferent to the emotional claims of the moment.

"Bon voyage," she said to him in a flat, tired voice.

"Thank you, Mom."

"Right," she said, and then looked pointedly out the screen door to the driveway where the cab was waiting.

"Well, I guess this is it, then." He stood in front of her in the hallway of the house he knew better, probably, than any structure in the world.

"Yup."

"And I'll call the moment I touch down," he said, leaning forward to sink his face into the familiar refuge of powder and warmth.

"Or not," she said, and he pulled away and looked at her in dismay. She was furious at his stupidity. The removal of her money, even though she no longer had any use for it, stung badly.

"Mom," he said again, "you know what? I'm not—I just can't leave it like this." He turned to the driveway where the cab was waiting and motioned to the driver that he'd be a little bit longer. Then he grabbed her gently by her elbows, where the flesh now hung in pleated folds over the bone. "C'mon back in," he said. "I want to talk to you."

"Talk?" she said. "Again?"

He took a deep breath. "Yes," he said, "again, imagine that."

He steered her back into the living room of the house and toward the couch.

"Here," he said, patting the tufted cushions. Shakily, on creaking haunches, she sat. He sat next to her and took her hands in his.

"You know," he said, looking into her eyes, "sometimes we just get carried away chatting about casual things. There's a time and a place for that, but this isn't that time. I have some things I need to say to you, right now, right here."

"Okay," she said, "so, say."

"I intend to," he said. "Number one, I love you, Mom."

It had to be said. It was also true. And declarations such as these had become easier to him after a year of life in Northern California, with its emphasis on sharing and caring and in particular, its men's groups where honest, forthright, hardworking guys wept in public like young girls. "I know," he went on, "that I was difficult at times as a child, but that's what childhood is, right, a place for kids to screw up? The mess I'm in now is entirely of my own making, but I will find a way out of it, just like I always do. From weak to strong, remember? I dance out to the very edge and then come shooting back. I *will* come shooting back. The most important thing is that you not worry and relax and enjoy yourself. That would be a gift not only to me, but most of all to yourself. Do you see that, Mom? Can you give yourself that gift?"

"John," she said softly.

"Yes?"

She paused, and frowned a moment, as if in receipt of troubling information. Then, lowering her eyes, she added, "I hope you recover the money. I know you need it, and your marriage needs it, and I—I—"

Her mouth stretching open silently, she made a soft *unh* sound, and then her head gently fell downward until it was resting on her breastbone.

"Mom?"

She raised her head and looked at him, her mouth still oddly open, and then lowered her gaze, directionally. He followed it, and both of them looked at her left hand, clenched now into a frozen claw.

"Mom?" he said more loudly.

She shook her head slowly with her mouth still open wide. No words came.

He jumped to his feet. "Can you hear me, Mom?"

She nodded slowly.

"Okay, here, lie down." He tilted her slightly backward on the couch, stuffing the space behind her with cushions. "I'll get you a glass of water."

She was shaking her head. He brought his head down near hers to hear.

"Ticky glug," she whispered.

He jerked his head back and stared at her. "What, Mom?"

"Hissle fazz," she whispered, while through her partly open mouth, he watched her tongue as it flexed like an undersea creature, unnaturally live and pink.

"You want what?" he asked.

"Sussy suff," she said and then she looked at him, her open mouth turning subtly downward in a frown.

"Mom," he said.

"Whoo?"

"I think you just had a stroke or something."

"No!"

"Mom."

"Tom?"

"What month are we in?"

"Muzzy might," she said, nodding.

He whipped out his cell phone and punched in 911. "Uh, I think I need an ambulance," he said, giving the address and then explaining to the bored-sounding operator that his elderly mother had suddenly begun talking gibberish. As an afterthought before he hung up the phone, he shouted, "And come as quickly as possible!"

There then intervened a strange period of white light in his head. From within that white light, he was aware of making her comfortable lying on the couch with her claw hand and her O-ring of a partly open mouth. He was aware of her being completely un- perturbed and even content—so it seemed—about what had hap- pened to her. Not long after, out of the edges of the white light, he heard the sirens coming.

"Mom," he said, "just lie still. The ambulance is on its way."

She nodded, her brow wrinkling quizzically. "Fancypants?" she asked.

The sirens grew in volume. There was a gritting of tires on the pavement, and a slamming of doors. He ran out onto the front stoop in time to see two EMT techs in blue twill uniforms step- ping out of the eye-catchingly painted vehicle in their driveway. The fronts of the houses around them suddenly came alive with twitching blinds.

"This the home of the little lady in distress?" the fatter of the two men asked, wheezing a little as he hefted what looked to be a big orange toolbox and climbed the three stairs to the door.

"Yes," said Potash, "thanks for getting here so fast."

"Speed for need," the smaller one said, coming up behind his colleague, "is what we do."

"Please come in," said Potash. "She suffered an I-don't-know- what."

The two men went by him into the house trailing a whiff of acrid body odor and medical disinfectant.

"Hi, sweetie," the big one said.

His mother, as best she could, smiled.

"Distension of labial cavity," the little one said out loud.

"Right," said the other, whose name, Lance, was printed on the breast of his uniform, "and we've got a little facial palsy and limb ataxia, I see." And then in a louder voice, "You feeling a little under the weather today, darling?"

The little one, Gary, ran back to the ambulance and removed from its back a gurney whose spindly legs sprang open, quivering as it was pulled free.

Lance whipped out a mike. "We've got a 9-12, mobile. We'll need some emergency attention at the ingress, on a gurney."

"Let's dance," said Gary, pushing the gurney lightly over the threshold of the house and into the room. The two men gently examined his mother, listening to her heart and taking her blood pressure while she blinked at them coquettishly. They then grabbed her and in a single coordinated heave swung her off the couch and onto the mattress of the gurney. As they began rolling her out of the house, she caught Potash's eye and gave him the cheerful wave and wink of a retiree embarking on a Caribbean cruise.

"Can I go with?" he called after the men.

"It's against the rules," Gary said.

"But you can ride behind us in your car," said Lance, and then craned his neck backward to add: "And shoot the red lights on the way."

"Thanks, guys." He locked the house behind them and watched as they carefully slid his mother into the back of the ambulance. The implications of what was happening were deeply upsetting, but Potash outwardly gave no clue to his feelings. Only, as he got into his mother's ancient car, which was so redolent of her that he felt nearly like he was *wearing* her in some way, he was suddenly consumed with blinding rage. He started the engine, which caught with a cough and then smoothed into an idle. He backed out of the driveway after the ambulance. It shot off down the street, and in the second before the siren began screaming, Potash had his first utterly clear thought of the day. The thought was that, though a peaceful man, he would hunt down Janelle Styles and stomp her to death with his shoes.

CHAPTER TWENTY-THREE

Margot's response was not long in coming.

Hi! she wrote. *I've been incredibly busy on a trip to points west and have barely had time for e-mail. I'm so glad we're on the same wavelength, dear Lawrence, and that your little temper tantrum was just that. Can I simply tell you that I've always been drawn to men of mastery and your work is genius, and gets to me? When certain people meet, the rightness of that meeting brings a ton of new truth to the table that they didn't even know they had till that moment. You're one of those people for me. I feel like my original self around you. I'm sorry to have had to resort to something like a letter to get in touch, but you hadn't answered my e-mails all weekend long and I guess I panicked! But in retrospect I realize I might have put you in a compromising situation.*

Where would you like to meet, my friend? And when?

Alone in the kitchen—he'd moved his laptop there in the hope of kindling some warmth for himself in the now-chilly-feeling house—Lawrence gave a long, sick, wheezing laugh and shut his eyes, calculating the exquisite terms of her future erasure from his life. He would do something—find some expeditious way to remove this woman—and the nastier the better.

Opening his eyes after this gust of feeling, he looked around in the hope of some small transformation in his situation. But the house returned his glance with the same cold impassivity as ever. The forty-eight hours since his wife left had been a trial. During the first day in particular, out of force of long-standing habit, he'd tried to call her several times, but her phone, maddeningly, rang on through, and it was suddenly borne in on him just how powerless a person is to make someone else love them when that other person either (a) doesn't, or (b) is withholding that love for reasons of being white-hot pissed.

In the meantime, when not actively engaged and on-task, he found thoughts of Glynis coming forward, in waves. She seemed in his mind to have assumed effortlessly the idealized status of a paragon; to be without flaws, Platonically perfect in every way. This process, first begun out of guilt during his initial flirtations with The Girl (he would no longer dignify her with her name), had deepened upon her departure, and now took the form of a long, closely reasoned argument, ongoing in his mind, which had as its object the undeniable proof that his estranged wife was the greatest woman he'd ever met.

Drumming his fingers idly on the kitchen table, he stared out the window, pondering his day. On a nearby sidewalk, a mother was half dragging two young children to school. As part of his training, Lawrence often thought in terms of evolutionary biology, and staring now at the mother—she was turning the corner toward the elementary school and still effortfully chivvying her kids—he saw not only a young woman immersed in the drudgery of her daily life but a human whose forebears had been naturally selected for their kindness toward their own offspring. A few million years of such winnowing had produced a coiffed, carefully dressed biped who was hardwired to make long-term sacrifices for her children, and thereby perpetuate the species.

One of the children, the boy, now tried to kick her in the shin, and she adroitly dodged him, and then shook her finger in his face. In terms of evolutionary biology, the world around us was a time-lapse film in which all animal, vegetable and mineral life was continually swelling in a vast crescendo of sorts—but toward what? What was the end result of those billions of blind alleys into which unsuccessful life-forms had stumbled and died en route to producing the pure, perfect inevitability of the world we knew? Was there an improvement, for all that work? Were we better than our arboreal forebears, with their browridges and haunted ape eyes? Terrifyingly more dangerous, infinitely more subtle, yes, but better?

The woman and her fractious children turned the corner out of sight, leaving him alone in the kitchen and returned to the glum particulars of his life. Until his wife left, he hadn't understood how crucial she'd been to providing a vibrant human current in the house. His hands were now no longer drumming on the table, but his mind was active, and hovering in nostalgic memory over the small caches of heat her body held: the twin dips of the clavicle, the webs between the fingers, the soft divots behind the knees. She had a potbelly, and her breasts sagged as if aligning themselves with the magnetic poles of the earth, and most of all, she was, to him, beautiful. The web of affinities they had slowly built around themselves had been shredded by a person whose motives—he didn't buy the "new truth" bullshit of her e-mail for a moment—remained to him still unclear.

He reread Margot's latest, just to confirm his disgust, and rather than respond, clicked off his computer, as if to stop the flow of her malignity. Then he got up, stretched his back, and decided to head out for breakfast. He went to the local diner, where in tribute to his wife's concern for his health, he ordered an egg-white omelette with spinach. He might thereby feel a little bit closer to her. A waitress with the immature milk teeth of a twelve-year-old girl served him, and he ate happily and felt content.

Fortunately, in service of his good mood, he had a new wave of bureaucratic things to attend to, and upon returning home, these consumed the rest of his morning. His book was being published in several foreign translations, which necessitated correspondence with well-intentioned English as a Second Language speakers who needed lexical mysteries ironed out. From Denmark: "Can you explain to us precise derivation of the phrase 'mind maze.'" From Brazil: "Please Mr. Billings be so kind to lend the hands, so that we can request from you the answer as follows: 'stare-down.' What is?"

He answered some more of these questions, and the rest of the day passed uneventfully, immersed in lakes of lost time in a state approaching dynamic inaction. At one point, noting happily some bills to be paid that were normally taken care of by his wife, he found saving cover for sending her an e-mail. He tried to be objective and businesslike for a few lines, but then his reserve melted, and he told her he loved her and missed her terribly.

Part of him was hoping to hear right back. But the afternoon planed silently and imperceptibly into evening, the sun shapes on the wall thinned and merged into dusk, and at a certain point, having mindlessly defrosted and eaten a pizza in front of a mindless television news show, he decided to write the girl back.

> *Margot, I'm pleased to hear back from you. I like the way you think. I'd like to propose that we meet in three days at the Orbis Restaurant, second floor. Dinner at seven thirty. How does this sound?*

After mulling it over, he finished with a very modest, *Love, Lawrence.*

Then he hit Send and whipped shut the case of his laptop so violently he was afraid he'd broken something.

Afterward, he felt too restless to simply stay at home. It was already evening, and he didn't want to feel himself prisoner of her eventual response, waiting on it like a supplicant. What to do? He decided to undertake something he rarely did. Go to a bar.

Lawrence was of the generation of men who liked to drink, though not usually in public. But on this night he got in his car and directed himself to the downtown area, where he parked, and strolled along the street, before darting into the loudest, most raucous club he could find. Stunned for a moment by the violence of the music, he went directly to the bar, where a couple of stools remained open. The bartender was young and handsome with high cheekbones and the lantern jaw of a born tyrant. Behind him were the ranked rows of liquor bottles, lit from below and glowing like isotopes. Lawrence ordered a gin and tonic, and then turned on his stool and, as if from a distant star, gazed at his fellow citizens.

Everyone in the mostly college-age crowd seemed still struck with the gloss of youth; still dewy and shiny, as if fresh minted. His mind in the grip of his evolutionary musings of earlier, he also saw how this biological scrimmage of high heels and bustiers, of muscle T-shirts and sexual bulges in clinging jeans, had the dead-serious function of perpetuating the genetic codes. Of course, these girls making themselves up for a night on the town in agonies of expectation—daubing bowerbird colors on their eyelids, and painting sexual emphasis onto their lips—had no idea that they were doing the vast, transpersonal will of their species. No, they were just getting ready to get liquored up and maybe get laid in the bargain.

Sipping his drink, he remembered how he and his wife had been spared this gaudy hormonal pageant. They'd met in that very brief period when he'd been working as a clinical psychologist, still terribly self-serious at the time, and she'd been a grad student seeking an internship. Relatively inexperienced in love, though already obeying the dictates of his profession that he appear to know everything, he was struck by how his conversation with her somehow passed easily through the grates of his newly self-conscious manner. Meeting her, he would later say, was like meeting his long-lost sister, the one who his parents told him had died in childbirth. Their ease together seemed anterior to their adult selves. Was familiarity finally the realest basis of attraction?

Lawrence drank his gin, munched on the ice in the glass, and gradually, as the relaxing power of the drink went through him, found himself trying to approve of the scene around him as a way of telling himself he was okay. This was an old and wily move of his mind, a psychic *redoublement* whereby he attached himself silently to a social setting and drew strength from the implication of his membership. In this particular case, he attempted to tell himself the raucous energy and optimism of the kids around him was in part *his* energy, and as such a corrective to that default to planetary pessimism that was so intellectually fashionable these days.

He ordered another gin and drank it slowly, savoring the thought. It was now a bit after ten P.M. and a huge new surge of bodies had pressed things to a natural bursting point. Conversation was nearly impossible, and people shouting drink orders were four deep behind him. It was about then that a sick, uneasy flare lit up the triumphal landscape of his mind. Glynis's friend Marley essentially lived in places like this. And if bars like this one existed for youth, then certainly a variant existed for the middle-aged as well, a bar in another part of the city, perhaps, where his wife and Marley might be seated right now, prospecting for the attention of well-heeled gentlemen.

Signaling to the bartender, he ordered a third gin and tonic. But he drank it quickly because, about halfway through it, he realized he was also growing tired of this place, with its strobing lights and deepening social roar. His little adventure, which had seemed a lark, nearly anthropological, an hour earlier, was becoming humanly a pain. He knocked the drink back, paid his bill, walked to his car and weaved his way home. It wasn't until he was back in his house, having fumbled with the key to the front door lock, that he announced to himself, "I'm drunk," and drunkenly opened his laptop. Among the many names stacked in his in-box, the girl's leaped out at him like something vignetted in a photograph. He clicked.

Yes, she wrote, *yes and yes.*

He slumped in his chair. His wife hadn't written back. Why was she being so frustrating, so pigheadedly wrong?

He sat there staring into darkness for a long while before going up to the bedroom. The room, because it had been the former scene of so many years of warm unthinking intimacy, seemed to him now to have the ambient chill of a meat locker. In the middle of it all, beneath its rumpled chenille spread, the bed lolled like a giant coated tongue. He undressed mechanically, lay on his side on the very far edge of the mattress with the distinct sense of teetering for an extended moment at the edge of wakefulness, waiting for something to save him, and was still waiting when sleep suddenly opened like a mouth and swallowed him whole.

CHAPTER TWENTY-FOUR

"Good morning, Margot," said Racquel, the lead therapist at the rehab center. She had a soft, droopy face, like something left out in the sun overlong, and a mole near her lips. Margot stared at the mole. She'd been at this place for five days.

"Morning," she said back, politely.

It was early in the day, and Racquel, who was enveloped in the chemical cold fruit smell of her shampoo, leaned forward.

"Where do you live?" she asked.

"Where do I live?" Margot repeated, and cued by the words, found herself remembering suddenly the warm spring day when she finally left her grubby communal hole on the Lower East Side and moved to her new apartment. She'd dropped her suitcases, spun around the living room, bent down to glimpse the dancing inch of the Hudson River visible between smokestacks from the corner window, gone and sat in the claw-foot tub, and then turned on the high-end Dacor oven just for the fun of it.

"744 West End Avenue," she said slowly.

"Great!" Racquel gave her a broad smile that made her mole, disturbingly, disappear.

She also remembered what was wrong with the apartment: she simply couldn't afford it. The magazine paid for a car service whenever she needed it; in moments of tipsy grandiosity with friends she could even fudge things and say she had "a car and driver." On top of that, hundreds of major American corporations fought for her time at work; they begged her for a little bit of attention; they spoke insinuatingly to her of the magic, aromatic junkets they'd like to send her on as Lulu Bach's assistant if she'd be willing to describe their goods and services in the magazine. In the antiworld of promotion, money flowed like rain, and Cachet was a pipeline to the demographic sweet spot of twentysomething girls with throbbing wallets.

But she was broke.

"And how long have you lived there?" Racquel now said, the mole popping back into view as her smile faded.

"Uh, maybe five years or so?"

She consulted a clipboard and then looked up at her. "You're doing just great, Margot."

"Am I?"

She was broke, yes, because though her job carried walloping social clout, she was paid miserably. At promotional events, poised and immaculate, she could be found lingering overlong at the antipasti table, and when home alone, often resorted to ramen or many-splendored omelets to get by.

"I'd like to talk a little bit about your last job," said Racquel.

She'd also begun getting invited regularly to a certain kind of party, an important party, of a certain quantifiable social mass, a party that was usually a module in some way of the parties thrown by Lulu Bach, with many of the same people in attendance, recycled through the long, self-renewing rhythms of the Manhattan social scene. She was establishing a reputation for a scorching wit hilariously at odds with her open ingenue persona, and people were beginning to take notice.

Many of those people were men. Not long after her arrival at the magazine, she'd begun dating, moving slowly but steadily upward through the lowlands of forgettable younger types toward that shining plateau where the wealthy older gentlemen grazed. These men were jaded by the deference shown them by young women but were struck by her slender prettiness and the disconnect between her sunny insouciance and her apparent fund of darker knowledge. She knew how to tweak them in their boredom. She knew precisely how best to sting them in their presumptions. Their surprise at her irreverence shaded neatly into erotic curiosity about the root source of her unshakable confidence, and they asked for her number and followed up.

"What did you last do for work?" Racquel asked.

"Uh, journalism?"

Within six months of her arrival in New York, she was already traveling in long, elliptical circuits through the inner dining rooms of some of the city's better restaurants, along with, occasionally, chartered planes and the bobbing foredecks of yachts moored off Seventy-Ninth Street. More than one of her gentlemen admirers floated the idea of a quick junket to Tortola or Mustique and took her back to his home, where, over drinks, he confessed himself intrigued by her seeming to know exactly how everything was supposed to go, down to the last detail. She laughed as she told a cereal magnate that his boardroom was "high-end Kmart." To a captain of industry she explained in sibylline detail why his decorator had committed a "punishable offense" by pairing ecru and taupe in the living room of his mansion. Sometimes these men took umbrage and went away and never came back. But often, they did.

"Can you tell me more specifically?" Racquel asked.

"I worked," she said slowly, "as an assistant to the editor in chief of a magazine."

Dressed in expensive off-the-rack clothes borrowed from the office, with a sheaf of business cards made up with the fanciful and importantly vague job description of "editor at large," she was out on the town, limiting herself always to a single drink, superalert, usually in heels, and gunning it, hard.

"I'm impressed by the clarity of your memory," said Racquel, tapping her pen on her clipboard and then signing her name on something. "This makes me feel more confident about our next move."

About six months after having arrived in New York, she hit pay dirt. Pay dirt was named Clive Pemberthy. Pay dirt was fifty-six years old, twice divorced, and richer not only than the men from the suburbs whose sole net worth was probably a town house in some satellite community of Manhattan (she could nearly smell the sick in the hallway from the puking babies); richer than the middle-aged accountants who sucked in their guts, told her they worked in "finance," and adverted vaguely to vast wealth available upon her compliance; richer even than the young analysts pumped up on a million-dollar year-end bonus and talking to her in a mix of dream speak and third-rate seduction about Cabo and Cancun.

She'd met him at one of the parties. She'd known he would be there and chose a dress off the rack at Cachet that gripped her body like a blown bead of superheated plastic. Arriving early, she put on lipstick at half-hour intervals, waiting for him to show. When he did, she followed at a distance, and at the moment he was first separated from his friends, she made her play. This she did by walking past him in a way that would allow her intuitively to feel when she'd "hooked" his eyesight with her hips, and then turning slowly on a heel while gazing at *him from under an arch of hair with a dawning recognition. He looked back, confused—did he know her?—and at exactly that moment she made a casually penetrating remark about a nearby painting on the wall.*

The remark, which had cost her twenty minutes earlier that day browsing in Wikipedia, delighted him to the point of outright laughter, before his watchfulness reasserted itself and he grew serious and asked her point-blank who she was. She told him, and after he digested the information, he told her that this painting was by an artist he happened to collect passionately.

Smiling, she floated her upper body out onto the air, cantilevering herself slightly forward off her hips, as if about to spring.

"Tell me more," she said.

Two weeks later, she was standing in his Italianate villa in Westchester, not far from the town of Katonah, looking out on seventy-five parklike acres that resembled a kind of spa. It was her first night there, she'd woken up before he did, and she now walked slowly down the central staircase, through the high-ceilinged main room and out the front door of the house. For a minute or two, she stood below the portico, looking out over the circular drive that hosted a variety of ice-cream-colored sports cars, a horse paddock, and beyond it, softly rolling hills leading away toward Manhattan.

Though she'd only spent a dozen or so hours in this house, she already noted that in the closet of his bedroom, behind his dress shirts and pants was a Gibraltar TL-15 tool-resistant safe, rated for an "attack time" of one hour. She'd observed that in a box on his dresser was a machine that wound his six watches—three Patek Philippes, two Rolexes and an Audemars Piguet—and that in the "aviary," as he called it, there was a collection of paintings that hosted, recognizably, a small Renoir, some Degas pen-and-ink drawings and a delightfully obscene Egon Schiele. Casually, she'd seen the domed closed-circuit cameras in the corners of certain rooms and had deduced from conversation that a new maid had just been hired. As well, she'd noted that his wallet was hanging in his pants in the unmonitored bathroom and that this wallet contained a thick green slab of hundred-dollar bills.

It was spring, and the morning air had a coolness to it. A plane droned by overhead, beginning to bank toward JFK. She notified herself that this impersonation of a kind of arch debutante needed to be interrupted; that she needed to assert the other part, the part that earlier that night had watched him gasping above her in emulation of something approaching a heart attack, while she pretended to something she didn't feel in the least.

Light as a gazelle, she scampered back upstairs. He was still sleeping, facedown on the bed, his lips pressed somewhat thickly against the pillow as if she were still rolling beneath him. At fifty-six, two orgasms were better than a Seconal. Today would be the maid's second day on the job. In the bathroom, Margot peeled several hundreds off the wad of bills in his wallet and slipped them into her purse.

There was a disturbance, a scuffling sound at the door, and Dan France burst into the room, breathing heavily, excited.

"Well?" he said.

Racquel turned to him with her mole entirely hidden by the force of the happy creases in her face.

"Good news," she said. "Our student is showing strong cognitive recovery. I'll be talking to her case manager later today, about setting up meetings with a nutritional therapist, and getting her familiar with working with a home health aide, prior to the move."

Racquel looked at Margot and said with mock exasperation, "We want you out of here!"

Then she turned smiling to Dan France, and added, "She's doing *great so far, and my prediction is that within a very, very short time, our Margot will be returning home, and maybe one day even taking up the life she had."*

"Imagine that," said Dan France, shaking his head in wonder. "I mean, just go ahead and imagine that."

Margot looked at him over the still-sleeping body of Clive Pemberthy, and behind him, the house filled with floor upon floor of wealth and privilege.

"I think I can," she said, smiling.

CHAPTER TWENTY-FIVE

His mother had experienced something called a transient ischemic attack. After an anxious night waiting while tests were done, Potash was at the hospital at seven A.M. sharp when the news was brought to him in the waiting room. The conveyor of this news was an unnaturally handsome doctor named Feyadh, the Iranian ("we prefer 'Persian'") resident. His mother had had a kind of ministroke, the doctor explained in his sweetly jumbled English, batting his doe eyes, but as was often the case, the condition had "self-resolved," and though it was a dark precursor of serious things to come, it had left no traces in its wake.

Potash felt relief the approximate weight and size of a log roll off his chest. Entering her room ten minutes later, he found his mother unsedated and sitting happily up in bed.

"Well, good morning," he said, unable to keep from smiling hugely himself. Her recovery seemed to him faintly magical.

"Don't act surprised. You think you were gonna get rid of me that easy?" The lines were vintage, but he noticed that she for her part seemed to be glowing.

"Oh, Mom," he said, shaking his head affectionately.

"I'll tell you what it was, " she said, and held a hand to her mouth like a mini-megaphone. "It was like a twenty-four-hour flu that turned off my talking power." She lowered the hand. "Snap, like that. But the important thing is that it turns out I have nothing wrong with me."

"Not exactly," he said, "but almost."

He moved over and, very gently, sat on the side of her bed.

"Well, happy to see you too," she said tartly. "What, you can't let your old mother enjoy her recovery? I feel fine, and so should you."

He smiled at her.

"You wanna provide me my laugh cues, Mom, and tell me when to cry, too?"

But she ignored that, and said simply, "Home, James! Momma can't wait!"

"I'll take you as soon as they say I can."

"Who they? Doctors? What do they know?"

"You really are back."

"You didn't believe me?"

"It was pretty scary."

"Well, I'm a tough old bird."

"Yeah, lots of sinew."

He laughed as she raised one hand in which she held the daily paper and slowly, with great care, swatted him on the head.

"For shame!" she cried.

They were both very happy.

On the way back to her house, having promised her he'd be back that evening around dinnertime, he called his wife. Though still vaguely despairing about the bigger picture, he was feeling some-what expansive in a local, under-the-circumstances way, and was all the more dismayed to meet with a sharp corrective to his fledgling good mood. His wife was worried. The children were "acting out," and the therapist Dr. Feibenbush said that the older child, Louis, apparently suffered from something called "video-dependency syndrome." This was a condition whose main symptom was an inability to tolerate more than an hour away from a computer screen bearing biomorphic, faintly dragon-shaped entities at war, or phenomenally realistic infantrymen plinking away at distant targets. Deprived of them, he'd become aggressive and unruly—too much, apparently, for a tenderhearted woman alone with him for days on end. To make things worse, she'd recently discovered a trove of gun and weaponry magazines in his closet, and for parents with male children of a certain age (as she'd already explained to him), Columbine was never far away. Her voice was teary, breaking up.

After calming his wife down by promising that when he got home in a few days he would take matters in hand and enroll his stepson in a martial arts program run by one of those flinty, warm-hearted ex-Marines with a reputation for positively channeling adolescent angst, they had a lovely few minutes together. She was deeply relieved to talk to him, and he for his part was fortified by the feeling of having exercised his masculine, not to mention professional, bona fides.

He pulled the car into his mother's driveway and set upon freshening things up for her imminent return from the hospital. It was now ten thirty in the morning, and when the phone rang from an unidentified California number, his first thought was: early riser.

"Hello?"

"Mr. Potash?" said a familiarly plummy, theatrical voice.

"Yes?"

"Wilbraham here. I hope this call finds you in good health."

"Ah, Mr. Wilbraham, of course. Uh, I'm fine enough."

"Good to hear. I'm calling," he announced dramatically, "to tell you the creature has been located."

Potash, who had been in the midst of nervously finger-combing his hair, stopped with his hand held crablike on the side of his head.

"You found her?"

"Not I, but Herve, my dear assistant and part-time bloodhound. She goes by a variety of names, our girl, and the inside word is that law enforcement is drawing up an indictment. Wire fraud, embezzlement, RICO statutes—the book, summarily, will be thrown at her. Herve tracked her down to a small hospital in New York City, of all places. My information"—there was a rustle of papers—"is that the creature is there due to an injury of sorts, and furthermore is currently under police protection. I needn't tell you all this makes her apprehension a quite formidable task."

"Yes."

"Quite formidable, yes," Wilbraham repeated, half to himself.

"Still," said Potash carefully, "this is great news, no?"

"No," said Wilbraham, "and yes."

"Why no?" Potash asked.

There was a pause, during which Potash could imagine Wilbraham massaging his soft, fleshy face with the palm of a hand.

"Friend," he began, "we are now arrived in the course of our relationship at what I like to call The Good Bad Place. Good because the malefactors have been found. Bad because now we're faced with what to do with that fact."

As was often the case with Wilbraham, Potash felt himself wanting to pierce the large, cloudy ball of words that seemed to rotate around the man. He said simply, "What now?"

"Indeed." Wilbraham cleared his throat explosively. "It goes like this, Mr. P. Police arrest criminals. Then prosecutors take cases to trial. Then juries convict, if in fact they do, and judges sentence. But that takes a long, long time. By that time, their booty, which is to say your ex-booty, has either been depleted by legal fees or, as is increasingly the case, is cooling its heels in untraceable offshore accounts. Does the name 'Canary Islands' mean anything to you?"

"Yes, I know all about my chances. Mr. Bortz was quite up front about them."

"Ah, the punctilious Mr. Bortz, of course. Well, that being the case, I have a modest proposal for you."

"I'm dying to hear it."

"No doubt, which is why I suggest the following: that you fly to New York and intercept the creature during a public errand when she leaves the hospital, as she no doubt shortly will. Supermarket parking lots, for example, are perfect sites for this. You surprise her when she is laden with foodstuffs and her guard is down."

"What?" Potash asked, and then again, "What?"

"You're impatient. You're incredulous," said Wilbraham. "I can't blame you. But please lend an ear. This story begins with you employing the services of a moonlighting deputy in your area who is a very good friend of mine named Edward Berke. Mr. Berke is an unusual soul, who is both amenable to working in the legal shadows, and, if necessary, not. With him riding sidesaddle in the car with you, you will not only be indemnified against violence, you will also have the full moral weight of the law on your side. He is fully armed with the various implements of his profession but he is in plainclothes. Are you with me?"

"I think so. And I'm already in New York, or in Connecticut, for my mother."

"Bingo," said Wilbraham sonorously. "To move on, then: you

arrive with Mr. Berke and at the right moment you leave the car and you intercept the creature in an open space such as this parking lot. Very quietly you explain to her that she has ruined your life. She is a sociopath, of course, so you quickly add that if she in any way wants to flee, Mr. Berke will have her incarcerated for a very long time. Now here's the important thing. Having leveled with her, you explain that if she accompanies you to your car and specifically to the computer there and initiates a wire transfer for the monies back into your accounts, you will drop all charges and chalk everything up to bygones. If she says she has already spent some of it, then you generously offer to allow her to keep that. In the money recovery business, we deal with percentages. During all this palaver, you adopt a tone of utterly calm exposition. You talk to her the way you would an errant kitten. You are firm but controlled. If she does in fact try to run, Berke will immediately give chase and apprehend her. Berke is quite fleet of step for a heavy smoker. If she runs, then the likelihood of your recovering your fortune will have statistically just leaped to a far shore. But on the off chance that she realizes you've effectively got her blocked in, she may just, as young people say, 'go with the program.'"

There was a pause. Potash heard himself breathing into the phone.

"I'll do it," he said immediately.

"Which 'it'?"

"Berke," said Potash. "I'll go with Berke. Can you have him call me?"

"Wonderful, my dear Potash." Wilbraham said. "I'll have him phone you promptly. Berke is very expensive, but then again"—he laughed his light, candid, utterly disarming laugh—"so am I."

And with that, five thousand dollars' worth of a retainer clicked off the line.

As soon as he could, Potash went upstairs to the study and began unpacking his laptop. He was eager to get Wilbraham's e-mail containing "the creature's" home address.

Waiting for his computer to boot up, he called Cas at his office. They'd had a general plan to meet, but Potash wanted to know if he could bump his lunch today, because he had something very special to talk about. There'd been, he added, "a break."

"Sounds promising," said Cas, who put him on hold for an unbelievably long time. When he got back to him, he said grandly, "You will be accommodated."

"Great," said Potash, "because this is gonna be good."

"I'm sure of that. And by the way, I have an in with some pretty high-level law enforcement types just now. What did you say the chick's name is?"

"She's got a barrel of pseudonyms, apparently. But all I've got is 'Janelle Styles' and the various wire transfer coordinates and bank records, which I can e-mail you. You know the rest."

"That'll do," said Cas, hanging up fast.

CHAPTER TWENTY-SIX

Four days slid by without his wife coming home. Four days during which the house itself, by some mysterious additive process, seemed to grow larger and looser around him, the ceilings higher, the inner spaces traversed by imaginary drafts. He had future classes to prepare, and an introduction to write to a friend's book. Yet he was stayed from these activities by a growing conviction that he'd made a mistake. Not only the mistake with the girl, but a larger life mistake, which accounted somehow for the vehemence of his wife's reaction.

What to do? How best to atone? Sometimes physical activity trumped all the intellectual delving in the world. The next morning, after breakfast, he cleaned the first-floor windows of the house with penitential precision, drawing Windex in shining arcs through the dusty glass. It was a choking, repellent job, but he did it. That afternoon, he tackled the crawl space. Located below the screened-in back patio, it was gross by anyone's definition. Wearing gauntleted gloves, knee pads, and a long-handled rake, he drew out mucky old newspapers, playing cards (it was probably a "fort" for a generation of children in the 1960s), a few small feral skeletons of field mice, ancient toys, and lots of rotting, smelly debris of inde-terminate origin. It felt like he was allowing the house to throw up.

After a shower, he went out and bought flowers. These he placed like splashes of color at the cardinal points of the living room, and he told himself that his wife would have loved the touches.

The fit of industry was hypnotic, self-sustaining. That same af-ternoon, he buffed the floors slowly, bending and straightening like a Venetian gondolier, while listening to the classical station on the headphones. A Verdi string quartet suppressed the skirling sound of the pads. When evening came on, he downloaded a Moroccan chicken recipe from Epicurious, then went to the local specialty shop and bought cardamom, kale and fenugreek. As the pot sim-mered on the stove, feeling himself transported to Glynis through the magic of olfactory memory, he called her. His voice was light and musical with self-satisfaction.

"Glyn," he said into her voice mail, "I'm cooking chicken Dji-bouti, and it smells wonderful and the house is sparkling. Every-body wants you home."

He was not a natural cook; he measured everything to the mil-liliter; made dinner like he was titrating chemical reagents in a lab. But the result—and he called her again, unavailing, as he sat in front of the table—was a miracle of refined cuisine.

He ate his spicy chicken and tried, again, to think clearly. A nat-ural list maker, he drew up one now, using a yellow legal pad and a fountain pen. It read something like this:

Good Lawrence:
Stable
Calm
Provider

Bad Lawrence:

Autocratic

Bullying

Conceited

Good Glynis:

Intuitive

Loving

Generous

Bad Glynis:

Plotting

Deflecting

Vindictive

But what was the use of thinking in these broad and silly categories? The truth, he knew, was found away from the orderly ruled universe of his yellow pad. The truth, unbeknownst to his wife, was that he'd had more—many more—than simply two "slippages." Lawrence's particular mental discipline took the form of absolute belief in his own story line, and of the presentation of himself as a diligent, fundamentally loyal man who lived in the sunny plateau of a good marriage. But this broad-strokes portrait was honeycombed with derelictions: repeatedly over the years he'd been unable to avoid the sudden flash of sexual interest in a woman, and repeatedly, he'd sought to satisfy it. He wasn't proud of this fact. He'd privately gone so far as to see a therapist over what he regarded as his "compulsive" and potentially "ruinous" behavior. Occasionally, in the aftermath of his flings, he beheld himself as loathsomely Janus faced: the one side humane, skeptical, progressive, and thoughtful, the other gross and inflamed; all sexual meat.

Lawrence's eventual answer to his quandary was to blame it mostly on them, his partners. To him they were like the succubi of classical myth, gorgeous, enticing creatures with a death-sting of seduction in their tails. Their wiles, after all, were infinite. Their gratitude at being granted the insight he had to offer was deep. Sex and curiosity occupied the same part of the brain. Who was he to lower the pedestal on which they placed his unique distinction?

But he was older now, and more mature. And part of that maturity consisted in the idea of deferring pleasure in the service of the greater good. Monogamy, after all, had a certain rough poetry to it. It spoke of the integrity of structures. Of the beauty of unmolested wholes. It spoke of clarity of purpose and fullness of intention. No, he'd have nothing sexually to do with Margot. She might have been beautiful, sharp, and as gifted a student as he'd ever known. But to sleep with her would be catastrophic. He knew it would.

The chicken, now half eaten, sat in the casserole before him with its ribs exposed like the scale model of a wooden boat. Beyond it, when he raised his eyes, he could see the wall calendar with his future dinner date with the girl circled in black, two days hence. He'd already been to the restaurant to look at it, study it, coolly consider the possibilities. It would be a master class in seduction with a nasty kick at the end. He would overrun her; crush her defenses; vaporize her self-control. And when he had her finally at his mercy, he would show her none.

Lawrence cleaned up, confident that his wife would be returning home soon, and that when she did, she would find a man renewed in spirit and self-corrected in his lacks. Afterward, he lay in bed, the bedside radio tuned to the divine intervals of Bach, and as the music bathed him with its sense of intricate problems gathered up, resolved and allowed to spill forth again, he felt a peace coming over him for the first time in days. He shut his eyes. The house, freshly cleaned, hissed from inside itself in a noise he chose to regard as contentment. The neighborhood spread around him in a series of warm, known overlaps. No enemy wanted his life. Lawrence aimed his mind at the future and entered unconsciousness like a man sliding triumphantly into home plate.

CHAPTER TWENTY-SEVEN

"New York, Chicago, and points north of Los Angeles."

"All of them?"

"Within a three-month span, John-O."

"Yeah, the wacky PI already gave me the big-picture read on her shenanigans. But how did you find out, Cas?"

They were seated at one of the dark-wood restaurants near Cas's office. Cas always dined in dark-wood restaurants.

"Ah, that's the mystery, isn't it?" he said. "Let me put it this way. Your girl is a hard worker. She dropped anchor in each of those places and I'm sure some now shirtless and probably pantsless bonehead can testify to that fact. No offense by the way. As for me, well, I called in a favor or two from some friends in law enforcement who were able to tap the resources of something called the BSA or Bank Securities Act. Even before the Patriot Act, you see, Big Brother was hard at work giving the American citizens a collective prostate massage in their checking accounts and surveilling the living shit out of them. Plus, I'm owed favors. *That's* how I knew."

They had roomed together in freshman year of college, and the two of them—a reserved, somewhat bookish kid from an Old Left middle-class family and the showboating scion of dynastic American wealth—had bonded over a shared joy in corrosive social irony and begun a conversation that, in a very real way, had never stopped since. Shared college histories, they'd discovered, trumped even the bitterest ideological divides.

Potash was shaking his head. "There goes that word again," he said.

"Prostate?"

"No, 'favor.' I mean, who doesn't owe you a favor? Sometimes I feel like I'm talking to Tony Soprano."

"You flatter me, my friend."

Potash looked at him as Cas dipped a piece of rosemary-studded focaccia in olive oil and asked, "And how's that bridge loan holding up, amigo?"

"Badly, thanks."

Tall, conventionally handsome, with a foxy crest of hair and skin boasting the ruddy glow of spa attentions, Cas said, "Foo!"

He whipped out his phone and punched a number. "Debby? Please disburse another 20k to my old footloose friend John Potash, would you? Same routing info as before. Yes, that's right." He looked at Potash a second. "No, it's better than that. Yes, he's still married. I'll tell you later."

He put the phone away.

"Thanks," said Potash, "a lot."

"Waiter!" Cas barked.

"Yes?" A gleaming young man approached at a race-walk from out of Potash's sight.

"We're celebrating my friend's discovery of the romance of poverty, and in that spirit, I was thinking a Super Tuscan, perhaps a nice Sassicaia to accompany our lunch."

"That sounds expensive," said Potash as the waiter withdrew, nodding.

"It is."

"I'm glad my fiscal ruin is an opportunity for you to let go."

"Bro, you're not offended, are you?" Cas looked at him with his sharp green eyes atilt. "Hey, I know you're suffering. But this is all in service of you getting your money back, remember? In the meantime, you're letting the witch win if you're having a bad time."

The waiter reappeared and harassed them with perfunctory sommelier courtesies that had to be acknowledged, rolling the bottle in front of them like an ancient artisan at a lathe, and making faces of the utmost concern as he decanted a few drops of it into a balloon glass for Cas's pleasure.

"Perfect," Cas said, with a small wave. As the wine pattered into their glasses, he went on, "Not that I mean to minimize what you're going through, Johnny. But you gotta allow me to have some fun while I run after you, cleaning up. You hungry?"

Potash lowered his eyes to the menu, but the fancy script looked like snarled string. He had no appetite in the least. "Not especially," he said.

"I'll order for you. Now tell me about your mom."

"It's like I already explained. Apparently a clot or fleck of arterial gunk can plug up a little vein in the brain for a few minutes, but then float away. Sort of like leaves over a storm sewer. It's scary while it's happening, but no damage—at least we think."

"Your mom was always tough as nails," said Cas, raising his wineglass. "Remember that visit sophomore year?" Potash raised his own for their second toast.

"Do I have to?" he asked.

His mother had shown up, taken opportunistic part in a parade against a nearby nuclear power plant, and in an ensuing scuffle with police had been photographed with a fifty-eight-year-old breast hanging out. The image had gone the pre-Internet equivalent of viral.

"May they only embarrass their sons to death once in a life," said Cas, and they both snickered as they drank.

"Speaking of near death," said Potash, putting his glass down, "the girl, the crook, Janelle or whatever her name is, apparently suffered a brain injury from an attack or something—they don't exactly know what. She's in rehab now but heading home soon. The noose is closing around her and an indictment is on the verge of being handed down. Meanwhile nutty Wilbraham the PI told me I should have a cop accompany me to intercept her somewhere and threaten prosecution as a way to maybe squeeze some money out of her. A Hail Mary, really, but what choice do I have? He even has the cop picked out. A moonlighting pal of his. I'm expecting his call later today."

"I'll have the salmon tartare," said Cas to the mysteriously reappeared waiter. "And my friend will have the spaghetti Bolognese."

"I will?"

"They make it wonderfully here, with a sauce of pork and beef that stews all morning. And you need something to stick on those skinny ribs of yours. But more important than your health is my next question."

"Which is?"

"Can I go with you instead?"

"Of who?"

"The cop."

"Absolutely not."

"I kind of need to."

"What do you mean, you need to?"

"Let me put it this way; I'm an asset, I'm your benefactor and I *want* to."

"How are you an asset?"

"Because I'm a star negotiator, John. I can do hard. I can do soft and teary. I can flow between the cracks. Besides," he said, leaning forward, "I could use a break."

"My heart bleeds for you. Putting the Gulfstream up for hock, are you?"

"Go ahead, laugh. But I'm serious."

"Cas, you'd be an impediment, God bless you, and besides, who the hell knows what types this chick is tangled up with? I mean, this could rapidly become something that isn't safe."

"Like the safari moment where the animals turn and rush the Land Rover? But that's exactly what I want!"

"You nut," said Potash affectionately, trying not to calculate exactly how much of his fresh twenty thousand would be instantly disbursed among ticking, overdue bills. Under reasonable circumstances, forty-five thousand dollars would be a sure buy-in to any adventure short of a moon shot. But now?

"Okay, you can participate in the stakeout with me, how about that? But the deal is I've got Berke on standby, and the moment we see the girl, we call him and he swoops in and deals directly, got it?"

"You, sir," said Cas, "are the straw that stirs the drink. And you won't regret it."

"I already do," said Potash, knocking back a glass of wine as tailored as a good suit, and winking at his old friend.

CHAPTER TWENTY-EIGHT

"Careful, please." Dan France touched her at the elbow and on the back as he walked her out the front door and toward the waiting car. She was wearing a lightweight dress, and she could feel the heat of his hands on her body. It was dusk, late summer. From every direction, the city appeared to fall toward her from incalculable heights. She paused on the sidewalk and turned one last time to behold the rehab facility. From inside, it had seemed to her an endless maze of linking hallways as big as the world, but now it looked simply like another Manhattan building turning a blind, boring eye to the street.

Then she was inside the car and sitting down amid the chrome bezels of the dashboard, dark-wood accents, and shiny surfaces holding a variety of subdued and blinking lights. Something pinged like a heart monitor.

"Nice car," she said.

"The Range Rover," he said, and his face held a rare light as he got in with a rustle of clothes, "is a thing of beauty."

The seat smelled of fresh leather. It smelled like affluence. She breathed it in, deeply. Dan France had already loaded up her few belongings in the back and they took off, driving slowly.

Over the previous days, her memory had crawled steadily forward, reclaiming past events. The process wasn't perfect. There was an indistinct stretch of time after Clive Pemberthy, in particular. She lived with someone for a while. A young someone. He had a nice house. Then one day there were shouts and cries. Somebody poured a drink over her head. She was kicked out, summarily. Not long after, she had sex with the married publisher of Cachet *and was eventually given a small settlement and fired. But against this story line an idea was forming. She remembered that it was an important idea, having something to do with her long-standing belief that she would join the wealthy ranks of her friends not by eating shit for a living, but as the result of an inspired leap, an act of levitation.*

"You excited?" Dan France now asked.

"What about?"

He looked at her and shook his head in mock disgust. "About going home, of course."

"Yes, I am, I think."

"You think? How about simply yes, for once? How about some simple good old-fashioned enthusiasm, huh?"

Instead of answering, she glanced out the window. Lights were coming on in the wall of high-rises running alongside the car, a million individuals flicking switches to turn dusk into day. In the somber stacked boxes of their apartments, people were getting ready to eat dinner and then fall asleep, dreaming dreams of spiraling flight, threat and sex, before putting on their professional clothes the next morning and riding down in elevators while giving no sign at all of having recently crossed vast, flaming landscapes at the speed of thought. The real reason we have faces, *she thought,* is to hold back what we're thinking from the world.

Dan France was now making a kind of mumbling conversation

that sounded like someone sharpening a dull knife on a wheel. She turned and looked directly at the squarish block of his head. She would use him as a perfect screen. And against this screen she would project the image of herself sitting alone in her apartment on that fateful day, recently fired from her job, her settlement already mostly spent on back rent and a fresh crop of new bills piling up. She'd been flipping idly through The New Yorker, *she remembered, when a small ad caught her eye.*

"Face and Body Reading for Financial Advantage," read the ad. It gave some particulars as to a seminar being held, along with a website, and a location, in a hotel about forty minutes north of Manhattan.

Hadn't she, she told herself, sitting back in her kitchen chair, already had a distinguished career of both reading and composing faces? After all, she'd faked Correct Schoolgirl. She'd faked Broody College Coed. She'd faked Perky Bright Journalist Ingénue. And, repeatedly, she'd faked Orgasmically Responsive Twentysomething. In all these roles, a quietly despairing voice had whispered to her that her charge in life was to keep up this particular appearance against all odds, because were she to waver even a little, it would mean to End Up Like Your Mother, looted by life, her husband and herself, in that order.

"What the hell is this?" Dan France said suddenly, looking into his rearview mirror.

"What?"

"A car, Margot."

"So—?"

"—That I've been seeing in our rearview mirror basically ever since we left. I just made some evasive maneuvers and he's still there."

"Maybe it's just a coincidence," she said.

"I don't think so," he said.

Before she could say anything in response, he floored the gas, a whomping mammal sound of blocked power arose from the engine, and the car shot forward down the road so fast that her head slammed back into the headrest.

"What the hell are you doing?" she shouted, as he wheeled the car in a violent spin that caused her now-gonging head to slew sharply around on her neck.

But he said nothing as they shot down a side street, roared into the air off a speed bump and then jounced heavily back onto the earth. Expertly he spun the large car yet again, pivoting seemingly on a single fixed point as the landscape wheeled screeching past the window, before the tires bit and they flew down a narrow, garbage-filled alley while scattering a spray of wooden boxes as they went. A few seconds later, with a sudden pitching forward, they slammed to a stop near the loading dock of a grimed warehouse. Dust, catching up to them, continued rushing past the car a moment.

She was hyperventilating. She was nearly in tears. But Dan France was the opposite of ruffled. He turned to her and said calmly, "I think it's time for a chat."

"You're insane!" she shouted, massaging her aching temples.

"I don't think so," he said.

"What the hell are you doing?"

"Uh, it's called 'getting away.' "

"From who?"

"I was about to ask you that."

"What are you talking about, Dan?" She felt as if a burning iron bar had been jammed laterally through her ears.

"I was going to have this conversation with you a little bit at a time once you got settled, but I think the time is now. You wanna level with me?"

"What?"

"Do you really think that I don't know what you're about, Margot?"

She looked at him in sincere confusion a second and then drew herself up.

"Take me back to the rehab facility, now!"

"Here's what I think," he said. "I think you've been involved in the game for a long, long time. I think you took me to be another mark, a rube who you could roll, but that you were too weak this time, too needy, and so the mask kinda slipped from the face. Am I right?"

She thought: should I do Indignant? But she felt too light-headed.

"I'll take your silence as a yes," he said. "And I won't be insulted by the fact that you treated me like I was an okey-doke who didn't know what time it was. You've probably always had one mental setting till now, and that setting was fraud. But here's what you don't know. I saw the other side of you, my friend. While you were lying there out cold in your hospital bed, I was digging all the way back to your poor crippled mother and the drunken fool who called himself your dad. Well, boo hoo on you, because we've all got a dozen cheap tearjerkers inside us and that's no excuse."

His face suddenly softened. "You're just lucky you're so goddamned cute."

She couldn't speak.

"And that I see the other person in you who you've probably hated your whole life long: the simple, fundamentally nice girl. Oh, and you're not going home either, by the way, if that's your idea."

"Why not?" she said, finally finding the words.

"Because whoever's tailing us knows where you live."

"But who would do that in the first place?" she asked.

They were pulling back onto a boulevard. "Gimme a break," he said, hitting the turn signal. "The list is probably as long as my arm." Up ahead she saw a sign for QUEENSBORO BRIDGE. She felt like throwing up.

"*Queens?*" she said.

He laughed, shortly. "*That's right, Princess. You've probably never been there in your life, have you? I'm taking you to a safe house we sometimes use for people we feel are under threat. You now qualify, I'm afraid. You'll stay there for a day or two while we figure out what to do next with you.*"

"*A day or two?*" she cried.

"*Try to control your joy.*" He turned to look at her, not unkindly. "*You'll have the guest bedroom all to yourself.*"

The expansion joints of the roadbed of the bridge were now rattling the car like so many taps on an inflamed nerve in the back of her head. She shut her eyes, and burrowed away from the horrid Dan France, and did her best to rejoin the recollection that was already in progress. If she looked hard enough, she could again see herself glancing at the Face Reading website, intrigued, and then booking a reservation. She could see herself entering the hall of the hotel in which the seminar was held. And she could see the man, the middle-aged facilitator of the weekend, calling for volunteers while she slowly, somewhat shyly raised her hand.

Margot opened her eyes and looked away from her own memories toward the mysterious dark borough of Queens. They had exited the bridge and were waiting at a red light. Dan France had fallen silent.

"I know," she said, "that you now think you know me. But you have no idea."

The light changed to green.

He laughed, but gently. "There you're wrong," he said, putting it in gear and driving away.

CHAPTER TWENTY-NINE

In their crappy rental car, gunning the gas as hard as they could, they'd kept up for a few blocks before losing him in the blazing traffic of the West Side Drive. They whipped the car onto the narrow shoulder and were giddily comparing notes on what they agreed was some kick-ass driving by a man who Cas insisted was "probably a mob wheelman," when the phone rang and both men made the exact same gesture of reaching automatically forward with their right hands. Cas laughed, but it was Potash's phone, and when he picked up, he saw it was his California home number. The idea of his wife sitting across the country in some quiet, sunny lake of light seemed faintly miraculous.

"Hi, honey. How's everything?" he asked, clearing his throat.

"I miss you." Her voice was plaintive.

"And I miss you, darling," said Potash.

"Where are you?"

"On Mom detail, mostly."

"And she's continuing to improve?"

"The woman is the definition of unkillable."

"Fortunately, she's also a sweetie."

Potash had never, not once in his life, thought of his mother as a "sweetie," but he only said, "She's hanging in there."

"Can I call her?" his wife asked.

"Of course, and she'd love that."

"Good, I will. You guys must have just finished up dinner, I imagine?"

"Uh, yes. Are we on speakerphone?"

"Sorry." Along with everyone else in their small town, she viewed cell phones as carcinogenic ray guns pointed directly at her sensitive brain, and she did her best to use a headset or speakerphone to keep the hostile waves at a distance. But she would indulge him. The background hiss changed registers. "Is that better?" her crisp, clear voice now asked.

"Yes, thanks, honey."

"So, I've been trying to plan our late summer trip." Anabella was a big believer in trips.

"Yes?" A tractor trailer boomed by with a frontal shove of air that shivered the little car.

"Gosh, what was that?" she asked.

"Thunder," he said impulsively. "It's thundering."

"Really? The boys were tracking you and they said the weather report called for sunshine tonight. Didn't you?" She had turned away from the phone.

"Right." She got back on. "John?"

"Yes, I'm here."

"Anyway, Napa."

"Napa?"

"Yes, for later this summer. I thought we could do a wine tour with the boys. They actually have some kid-friendly wineries, if you can believe that. The boys study the chemistry of fermentation and then we drink the fruits of that chemistry."

"Not cheap" was all Potash could muster.

"No, probably not. But within our budget, I already checked."

"Right," he said, the word costing him an effort.

"You okay?" she immediately asked.

"Uh, yeah, why?"

"You sound a little distracted."

"That's because I am."

"Of course you are," she said.

"Yes. And uh, here," he said abruptly, because he was sick of being slowly backed into a growing lie, "is someone who wants to talk to you." Frowning, he pressed the phone into Cas's hands.

"And how is my favorite *muy linda señorita*?" said Cas smoothly. Once rumored to have been in line for an ambassadorial post, Cas owned the outsize suavity of someone whose forebears, going back several generations, had never once taken out their own trash. As his friend bantered on, Potash looked out over the dusky highway, where the dotted snakelike trail of cars twisted toward the lit twin tiaras of the George Washington Bridge. At that moment, the busyness of the world felt vaguely an affront.

"Yes, and I'm glad to hear your voice, too," Cas was saying. "I'd just been asking about you and those adorable boys."

Cas caught Potash's glance and rolled his eyes.

"Are they?" he said. "Well, it's the age, Anabella. It's the age, and there's nothing to do about it. By the time they realize how grateful they are to you for what you've done, you're half dead." He laughed, nodding and said, "I know!"

He nodded some more.

"Good," he said. "And you to them. Maybe Cancun or Belize

this winter, en famille? I'd like that." And then, after a moment, again winking at Potash, he said, "Bye."

He hung up and said, "Your wife is a treasure, and you don't deserve her."

"Go fuck yourself," said Potash affectionately, dialing Berke, the cop, and swinging back into traffic.

CHAPTER THIRTY

Lawrence had already ordered a bottle of wine when he saw her enter the restaurant. She was wearing a tight black skirt, heels, a form-fitting top and above it, the helmet of close-cropped blond hair. And yet, despite her outwardly polished look, he was instantly struck by her air of subtle indecision. She looked like she'd dressed herself for a seduction she didn't quite believe in, and these mixed messages produced in him, dismayingly, a wave of sympathy for someone he sincerely believed to be among the worst people he'd ever met.

With a smile and a little wave hello, she approached across the floor with a sidling stride that gave the impression of wanting to draw near and flee at the same time.

"Lawrence, hi!"

He leaned forward and was surprised to discover that his heart was racing.

"Hi there. Long time no see," he said calmly.

She was closing the gap to his face with hers, and then pressing her lips on his. He made no effort to kiss back; but neither did he withdraw.

"Years!" she said loudly, pulling away and then giving him a false, asymmetrical smile while he registered the chemical fruit taste of her lipstick. "You look well," she said.

"You too."

The smile widened, though the eyes remained cold and flattish, studying him. She fanned her face with a hand. "Is it hot in here, or am I just nervous?"

"It is a little warm in here, actually."

"And I *am* nervous." She laughed.

"How about a little wine?"

She sat down, nodding, while he filled her glass. Though in his revenge fantasies of this moment, he had regularly dealt her staggering rhetorical blows and piled on viciously, all he now said was, "And catch me up on how you've been in the meantime."

She raised her glass and clinked his. "I will. Cheers, Lawrence."

"Cheers," he said, and they drank.

"Muuuch better," she said, exhaling even as her shoulders remained tensed and vigilant, "and the short answer is fantastic."

"How so?"

"Business has been booming, for one."

He looked at her. "You know," he said, "it occurs to me that I don't know exactly what you do. Your business card said only 'editor at large.'"

"That was from another life," she said airily. "Lately, I've been bouncing around a bit in finance."

"What end of it?"

"Can we not talk of it?"

"Of course." He shrugged his shoulders.

"It's just so booooring. Plus, there are more pressing things to talk about, like my apology."

He furrowed his brow. "For?"

"That absolutely crazy letter I slipped through your front door. Afterward, I realized that it was really and truly nuts and I am sorry."

"Thank you."

"And dangerous, too. I kept asking myself, why is this man preying on my brain so? I mean, I know"—her color was deepening and a flush had begun to spread upward over her breastbone—"that you're wonderful, and that your teachings and work gave me the confidence to strike out on my own, with great results, but why was I like"—she made a goofy grin and unmade it—"so obsessed with you?"

"Obsessed," he said calmly.

"Yes, and then, when I was getting on a plane in Chicago, it came to me."

She drew herself up and subtly pulled back her shoulders to raise the shelf of her breasts into his line of sight.

"You're hot."

He laughed out loud.

"What I mean," she said, her color deepening further, "is you're hot in this Distinguished Older man way that's not always so obvious. But when someone keys into it, look out!"

He floated onto his face a smile he called the Chaplin for how the raked cheekbones produced an off-putting wall of affect, and said, "I appreciate the uh, sentiment. But that's not how I think of myself."

"But that's what makes it even more so. Don't you see?" she asked. "It's what people don't say, don't do, don't belong to that makes them interesting. You've got this mysterious fund of knowledge and you know what makes people tick and yet you seem like you're thinking only of higher things, which is kinda irresistible."

She gave him what he judged to be the first credible, full-faced grin of their acquaintance, and then, dropping her voice, asked, "But are you only thinking of higher things, Lawrence?"

"I guess we'll find out, won't we?"

"Can I have some more wine?"

He laughed with a pleasurable release from the abdomen. "Of course."

As he poured her a hefty glass, he saw a nearby waiter looking at him with raised eyebrows and nodded at him to approach.

"Right," he said to her briskly. "Shall we order?"

She looked around. "Can you do it for me? Something seafoody? I think I'm getting drunk."

"Not a problem."

The waiter interposed himself, and rattled off the dishes in rapid Italian. Lawrence quickly made the choices and handed back the menus.

"You'd make a good husband."

"That's nice of you to say," he said, remembering that one of his persistent fantasies for this evening had been of enticing her into the erotic equivalent of those forest-floor traps lashed to a sapling that cinches tight around the victim's foot and then flings her in a high, bone-breaking arc into the air.

"You take care of the people you love," she was saying, "and I can tell."

The Chaplin floating firmly in place over the next few minutes, he did a lot of refilling of her wine while she continued talking. She liked to drink and she liked to talk, though he wasn't certain which came first, but his sense was that her inebriation, anyway, would help his cause. They'd arrived at the bottom of the bottle when two waiters swept in with a rolling cart and in a moment of smooth orchestration individually withdrew chafing dishes to serve piping hot spaghetti al cartoccio. This involved presenting a large paper bladder of a sort that when incised with a knife emitted a long hiss of steam. From within it, a glistening wealth of seafood and pasta tumbled out. The two of them were transfixed as the waiters expertly divided and served the dish.

Before the waiter left, he ordered another bottle. Though she wasn't yet slurring her words outright, he could hear a faint jostling at the bottom of her normally precise diction and a newly emphatic tone as she lit into her latest subject: the stupidity of men.

"Because men are stupid, aren't they, Lawrence?" she said giving a tentative stab at her pasta. "Not individually, of course, but in the aggregate, as my college professor of statistics used to say. Don't you think? It's like cats. Are they smarter than dogs?" She forked the food into her mouth, and slightly muffled but undeterred went on, "Oh, I know, all the bleeding heart animal liberation types won't say so, but we know in our hearts the kitty is a sharper beast, don't we?" She pressed the shiny fork to her breast. "And don't we know that most men in the world are as dumb as pails of dirt?"

"I'm not sure I ever thought of it quite like that," he said.

"Petty, cheap, vain, brittle, oh, and obvious. Men are obvious. Present company waaay excluded, of course."

"How so?"

She looked at him a second, and for the first time that evening, raised the wine bottle and poured herself another wine. "Sexually," she said.

He cleared his throat. "I gather you've formed strong opinions on the subject," he said.

"Over a lifetime of—oh, God." She clapped a hand to her mouth. "I *am* drunk."

"So what?"

"So now," she said, "you have no excuse left." She smiled at him. "To . . ."

"To not take advantage of me, of course."

Always, he recalled, it happened this way. Like real lightning suddenly flashing from a painted sky. A jolt of adrenaline had already turned him wakeful, but he deliberately made his features slack, good-timey, even a little sleepy, and said, "The thought had occurred."

She laughed uproariously for a second, and then got somewhat shakily to her feet, drawing herself up. When seated across the table from him, she'd been crunched in a posture of confiding intimacy, but as she stood up now, he was again reminded of her formal properties—breasts, hips, legs. He tried to look at her with the value-free equanimity of an entomologist would a bug, but lust fogged the lenses of his detachment and in a slightly alarmed voice, he said, "What are you doing?"

"I," she said grandly, "am going to the bathroom to powder my sobriety. Back in a jif."

CHAPTER THIRTY-ONE

In the dark, the house with its tall peaked roof resembled a witch's hat. The windows were covered with frilly sheers and the driveway was a humped pour of macadam that glistened in the streetlight like a pair of new shoes. To the letter, it was the kind of tidy working-class home that she had staked her entire life on avoiding. They were greeted by an odor as they moved slowly up the front brick staircase that he identified as the housekeeper's cooking.

"That's meat loaf," Dan France said, as if introducing her to a person.

And then they were inside, and she was sniffing the deeper closed odor of the house, which she recognized as belonging intrinsically to Dan France and which gave her the not especially pleasant sense of having traced a person's smell back to its source. Slowly she lowered herself to a couch. He was standing in place with his hands on his hips, watching.

"Drink?" he asked.

"Is that a verb or a noun?" she said softly. "Water, please."

He snorted, but appreciatively, and then left. The ride back had been a tense, odd twenty minutes in which he seemed to be looking at her from a newly ironical place that allowed him to be both warm and detached at the same time. It unnerved her. She glanced now at the nonworking brick fireplace and the whitewashed walls filled with travel posters advertising the delights of Barcelona and Paris, along with the lone potted plant, the woven carpet, the large flat-screen television and the basket on a gateleg table filled with what looked to be lifeless, possibly wax fruit, and she thought: I've gotta get out of here.

He reentered the room, with a tray and pitcher, saying, "And so?"

"What?" she asked.

As best he could, laden, he shrugged. "You know, the house?"

"About 1910," she said.

"Excuse me?"

"It was built."

He laughed delightedly. "Spot-on! You knew that?"

"Is this a safe house?" she asked. "Or your house?"

Silently he placed the tray and pitcher on a nearby table. Then he looked at her as if gauging her for a moment. "It's a safe house, all right," he said, "but I do occasionally use it when no one's here."

She stared at him.

"It belonged to a well-heeled crack dealer who went away for a long time and had everything impounded, including"—he gestured— "this. The house is the fruit of one of the largest interagency seizures of cocaine in New York City history. You may think I'm joking, but I'm not. Actually, what happened was . . ."

And at that moment she mentally stepped away from the amiable, country-smart, potentially dangerous Dan France and let him run on without listening. In accordance with her long-standing habit, she tuned him out. Her eyes focused on his face, which was presently drawing itself up into great, round shapes of animation while she stud-

ied mental escape routes. These weren't literal escapes out of the safe house, but the larger escape back to herself, which, it occurred to her, had been on her mind ever since she'd regained consciousness in the hospital.

"You know," she said, interrupting him, "I'm really tired. Could I lie down?"

"But of course." He sprang to his feet. "Sorry to sit here talking your ear off. Right this way." And hefting her bag, he set off down the hallway, while she followed. Presently they were turning into a small, chill, dark-wood space.

"Your room," he said. "Wait!" he cried suddenly. "I forgot the chair." And spinning in place, he race-walked out of the room, bringing her back a kind of Morris chair, which he held easily over his head and then set down on the narrow strip of carpeting by her bed.

"Here you go."

"Great."

Gingerly, saying nothing, she sat down on the chair, placing her hands on her knees. Without warning, a sudden memory made her tremble. But not with unhappiness.

"You know what?" she said. "I'm really beat, so if it's not too big an imposition, would you mind if I lay down for a nap now?"

"Not in the least." He brought his hands together in a gesture of satisfaction. "Meat loaf in an hour?" he said. "We need to eat early because I've got to get back to the city."

She nodded and he withdrew. When she lay down in bed, she was exhausted but far too excited to sleep. She was excited because the same memory, now widening in a starburst in her head, was casting a sharp, thrillingly detailed light over the next twelve hours. She understood exactly how they would go. Following her nap, she would have a slow, boring dinner with him, interrupted regularly by his magpie *chatter about the two dullest subjects on earth: his life and prospects and her future. He would embroider this with regular darting comments about her lurid past and she'd dutifully allow as how she'd been misled by people along the way, and in the process, make him feel the secret reason for her deviation from the good had been the lack of someone as manly and true as himself in her life. Showing humility and excusing herself as early as possible, she would return to her bedroom, brush her teeth, and afterward, lying down, let the universe spin her to sleep. The next morning, awakening in the cheerless borough of Queens, she would open her eyes feeling rested, and with some of that same orbital motion still at her back, put her feet on the floor and walk step by step into her beautiful new life.*

CHAPTER THIRTY-TWO

Berke called while Potash was making his mother's lunch. She'd returned from the hospital like an African queen on a barge, bearing a new, slow deliberateness that only underlined her essential pugnacity. He had helped her into the house, aiding her in the endless procession up the front stoop, and then held her hand while she sat down in sections, like a dynamited building collapsing, on the living room couch. He'd then gone to prepare her lunch and was shaking a canister of raisins into a bowl when his phone rang.

"Ed Berke" came the voice, without preamble, fatigued and full of authoritative police gravel. Potash felt a pang. Instead of calling him as arranged upon first spotting the girl, he'd instead pursued her with Cas, and by the time he did call, he had lost her entirely. Not that this lessened the exorbitant fee Berke charged him for being on standby.

"Bad news, Mr. Pootush," said the cop. "Since we last talked I reviewed the case and I'm not gonna take it. There's departmental heat like a blowtorch around this lady, and maybe even another officer involved, and that makes it a no-go. My advice? Cut your losses and forget it. That's all there is to it from where I'm standing. I'm sorry if this puts you out, but good luck. What I'm gonna do, since you're a good guy who got clipped pretty badly is, I'm gonna tell you something I'm not supposed to. You didn't hear it from me, but the address you can find her at is 5775 Ocean Boulevard, in Queens. But I wouldn't go there if I was you."

And Potash, who for the rest of his days would remember that he was staring at a watery bowl of raisin-dotted yogurt when blindsided by the news, said only the word "Okay!" but softly, and after muttering something in closing, hung up. He wrote down the address, and then, unable to process fully what had happened, decided to revisit it later, from the far side of pretending nothing was amiss, and so continued methodically for another two minutes to prepare his mother's lunch. But he was no longer entirely in his body. In fact, he wasn't even *near* his body. From halfway across the room, he watched himself leaving the kitchen and then bending down to the large, recumbent person who seemed to smile and then frown without context, while he said, "Here ya are, Mom."

He watched the person say, "Thank you," but somewhat automatically, and then reach a veined hand toward the television remote control. A moment later, with surprising fluidity of motion, he watched the person stab a spoon into the mixture he'd prepared while with the other hand clicking rapidly through the channels till stopping at the image of a political discussion show involving middle-aged men sneering at each other in stage makeup. "Ah, but it's good to be home!" she cried.

"I'll bet," he said, entirely without conviction.

He left his mother to her meal and over the next minute wandered aimlessly through the house till he fetched up in his bedroom. Standing there in a light trance before the familiar slants of light and shade, and the furniture and knickknacks unchanged for twenty-five years, he felt as if his childhood had already outlived him somehow, and through the agency of these books, toys, deflated footballs and folded baseball mitts was now signaling backward in time from the future with the message: We tried, John. We gave it our best shot.

And we lost.

Frowning, Potash sat heavily down on the small bed, while a faint odor of something sprang up into the air about him, a shower of ancient scent, expressed into the atmosphere from the mattress after a twenty-year dormancy. For more than a year, he'd been living in a bright, supershiny soap bubble of certainty about his prospects, flush with happiness, deeply in love, and moving, as he believed, from strength to strength. All that had been brought to a swift end by him allowing money, that magic water, to run through his hands till there was no more.

Potash took those same hands and covered his eyes with them, shutting out the world. Was it the narcotic influence of love itself that had made him this dumb? Or had he somehow been defanged by sunshine, New Age babble and ocean views? Where had his street smarts gone, anyway? And where the protective belt of thick, tough cynicism on which he'd always prided himself?

There was only one thing to do. He passed the rest of the day on a version of automatic pilot, keeping up appearances with his mother and making her her dinner. Having arranged for a home health aide to come calling the next morning, he took a sleeping pill to knock off early, and seven hours later, while it was still dark, he awoke and slipped out of the house and into the garage, where he started his mother's car and headed, alone, for Queens.

CHAPTER THIRTY-THREE

They'd finished their dinner in a riot of innuendo, having quickly polished off the second bottle of wine. It came back to him so easily, this warm, aerial art of flirtation. Always, it was the woman petitioning him from afar. Always, it was her signaling with her eyes and breasts and the cant of her pelvis that she was open, interested. Invariably, with a certain staged reluctance, it was him admitting to being swayed. To being slowly convinced, and drawn into the physical particulars while appearing elsewhere engaged. The lounging, roundabout trip to bed was his specialty. And women, after all, had this way. As for Margot, he was merely softening her up while waiting for the moment to strike as hard as he knew how.

In the service of this eventuality, he ordered brandies after dinner. Brandies were a man's drink, a burning distillate made to be absorbed into yardages of sinew and fat. To his disappointment, however, she demurred, merely taking a sip and putting it down. He threw his down the hatch and ordered another. Not long after, by common consent, they left the table and proceeded out to the lobby. Slumped giggling together, they rode the elevator to the top floor because she wanted "some air."

Then they were spilling out of the elevator and onto the carpet, whose mix of turning circles and barred slashes gave him the feeling of a recurrent mood disorder.

"This is . . . bad," he said gnomically, and they exploded in laughter.

"What you haven't learned sufficiently, dear Lawrence," she cried, "is that bad is the new good!"

The upper floors of the hotel, which dated from Victorian times, were rarely used, and to conserve electricity, were lit only sparsely. Her face, as it drew near his, was greenish gray, a bit feral, somewhat indistinct. But then again, the frames of everything were shuddering and twisting and wreathing in the dimness. Perhaps he'd drunk more than he'd thought.

"To the roof!" she cried.

"Wonderful idea," he said, thinking that if nothing else, the cool air of evening might bring him around a bit, and would also give him fresh opportunities of some sort. *I must*, he thought, *get her into open ground*—though what he would do with her there remained still unclear.

In one corner of the hallway a long staircase drew upward to the roof. Once, according to local legend, a ballroom had been fitted to the rooftop garden, and this staircase, with its sweeping, double-width proportions and enormous vertical rise, now had the air of a defunct colossus; a massive output of travertine and marble leading to a small, latched fire door at the top.

"Wow," he said as they glimpsed it.

Then they were sweeping forward, arms around each other, and in a single rush, flowing up the stairs. Very clearly, he could feel her body through the press of her ribs against his. Obviously, he reasoned to himself, the moment was drawing near. He couldn't feel his legs, especially. It was a marvel to him that she was able still even to stand.

They made it to the top. He was getting ready to press the metal bar to allow them access to the roof when her hand on his forearm stopped him in mid-gesture. Her eyes, which had been somewhat slack, drew suddenly to a sharp focus.

"We've come to that part of the night," she said, "where I get to ask you something."

He looked down modestly at the ground. Over the years this particular bridge had been crossed by women with florid declarations, with whispered confessions and, several times, with coldly clinical requests for sex. Who was he to deny them? Life was hard and people required comforting. He made a pushing movement of his teeth into his lips that signaled his patient willingness to entertain all inquiries.

"Are you happy with your annuities?"

Lawrence laughed out loud. So she was going to make a joke of it? Fantastic! He turned to her with a smile.

"You're funny," he said, again touching the wall slightly to keep himself upright. But she was merely eyeing him with the same flat, neutral stare.

"You've had two books each on the *New York Times* bestseller lists for nineteen weeks," she said calmly, "and you bought your house in 1984 for three hundred and fifty thousand dollars. I'm betting you've got a tidy pile stashed away, Lawrence. Are you really satisfied with a future of safe, minimal returns?"

His hand was on the bar to open the door to the roof, but he never pushed it. Through the fog of his inebriation, a worrisome signal reached him.

"How," he began, "do you know about——"

"Your books?" she said crisply. "It's my business to."

"Now, wait," he began, "just a——"

"Lawrence," she cut him off impatiently. "Waking up old money is what I do. And research is a part of that. The question is, Can I wake up yours?"

For a moment, the erotic subtext of her words reassured him. But her bright, composed face in front of him read as anything but lubricious. He again grew confused.

"Think how great it would feel," she was saying, "to have your money making you a fortune instead of being parked on life support in the annuity nursing home."

He touched his mouth experimentally. His entire face had a poured-in feeling. "But why," he asked, "now?"

"If not now, when?" she said sensibly. "Why are you giggling?"

Why was he giggling indeed? He'd begun giggling because he was getting really drunk, firstly. But mainly he was giggling because for all this time he'd been under the illusion that her interest in him was erotic while it had been strictly, boringly, plainly commercial. She was after his money! Was this possible? Could he even remember the last time something like this had happened to him?

"Well," he said, "I really appreciate your interest in my fiscal, uh, well-being, but the fact is I'm set up fine. I've got state municip . . ."—he struggled with the words—"municipals that net me four percent."

She drew away from him a moment. "I can get you eleven," she said, "even in a down market."

The Chaplin still wobblingly in place, he looked at her while trying to arrange his thoughts. He had agreed to this meeting in the hopes of rooting this dangerous person forever out of his life. Delusionally, as it turns out, he had taken her self-interest in his money to be erotic interest in his person. And yet even as recently as an hour or so ago at the restaurant, she'd been filled to the brim with flirtatious badinage and showing him her body, wrinkling her nose, and sending him warmly inviting waves. Slowly, with drunken care, swaying at the top of the stairs, he drew an erratically straight line between these two points: drunk and flirty before, sober and professional now. There was currently about her no entrée that would have allowed him a devastating conversational blow, knocking her forever out of contention. He was without the necessary erotic traction.

"Bioprocessing," he heard her say. He was nearly disbelieving. He looked as if through a long, bending telescope at the close-up of her mouth. The puffy wing-like sections of her lips were moving in rhythmic unison. These lips were animated by the power of her breath. He was now drunk enough to be seeing things in the knobs and sticks fashion of alcoholic reduction. Everything was suddenly clear. She had beaten him at his own game, outflanked his ability to read the subtler human signs in the service of a deeper truth. Though he'd known she was a player and a phony, he'd underestimated her brilliance at both.

"Depreciation," he heard her say. She would never stop talking. She was young, strong, as smart as he was, and she had her whole life ahead of her. Plus, she was beautiful. There was really nothing else to be done. He was still nodding in apparent agreement with her conversation as he reached forward, expressionless, and pushed.

CHAPTER THIRTY-FOUR

After locking her in for the night, Dan France returned early the next morning, while it was still dark out. She was already up. The high-toned lecturing began with watery coffee not long after and continued, to her dismay, for an hour straight. The lecture was delivered in the little kitchen, accompanied by the hectic sound track of kids heading toward school on the street outside the windows. Righteous and scolding, it had about it the unvarying grate of a chain saw. Over the course of their friendship she'd gone from being a victim to a perp, for all intents and purposes. Yes, they were closing in on the person they believed had assaulted her, but that didn't change what she herself had done to at least a half-dozen people, according to their records. And she was too talented to do this. And good, too. Deeply, humanly good, in the heart, where it counted.

Did she know that the FBI had partnered with not only one but several U.S. district attorneys, and that an indictment for wire fraud was about to be handed down? She did Shock at him, seasoned with a touch of openmouthed Horror. Did she know, he went on, nodding sympathetically at her evident distress, that sentencing guidelines in a case like this, even with no priors, called for a substantial time away? Now, he couldn't promise, but by pulling some strings with a friendly prosecutor, and factoring in her full cooperation, he could probably get her off with a probationary arrangement, or minimum (he stressed that word) jail time. The great, round shapes of happy animation blew up all over his face again as he began urging her to agree that it was a blessing she'd been caught, because from here on everything would be different.

"Caught?" she said, quietly.

But either he didn't hear her or he simply missed her intended irony by a mile, because now, his voice beginning to fill with the wind of his convictions, he began to explain that, if she were in agreement, he would take her on as one of his most important projects in life. And he loved projects. He loved rebuilding things that were skewed or mismated or crooked in their parts. Making stuff whole was what he did. He ministered to it from his "heart," which he allowed her to imagine as a righteous machine whose powerful pistoning single-handedly upheld the fallen of the planet. He was a "throwback" of a sort, and descended from a "long, interminable line of do-gooders." She was a "hard nut to crack," but he believed in her because he'd gotten to know her and know her story. Smiling at her now, he spread his arms wide in the manner of a preacher exhorting his flock.

"Understood?" he said.

"I think," she said, "this is the part where I get to say thanks."

"You're welcome," he said. Stirred, breathing heavily, he went on, "As I said, I know someone whose nature is kind, even if she grew up wrong and got some switches flicked by her parents that shouldn't have been. And what I said to you in the car about you having just another hard-luck childhood? I lied."

She looked at him.

"It wasn't just another," he said. "It was special. It was yours."

"To my knowledge," she said, "my parents didn't flick a single switch."

"Very funny. You know what I mean," he said, and then sitting down next to her, he bent close, blew a moist, minty fog of breath in her face and kissed her on the lips.

It was not an especially interesting kiss; it reminded her of the bashful quick kisses of high school boys that faded off the face like breath off a mirror. But as he drew away afterward, and looked at her shining-eyed and with a crooked little smile of triumph, it occurred to her she was seeing him in what was quite possibly one of the happiest moments of his life.

"I've wanted to do that," he said, "for a while now."

"Did you?" she said, and in the moment of silence that followed she realized the previous sounds of children en route to school had vanished, swallowed up by subways and buses. Everybody had somewhere to get to in the world; half of life was getting to that place as quickly as possible. Where did she have to get to? Dan France had now begun talking rapidly, as men sometimes did after first kisses. He was composing that familiar aroused-guy music of peppy, upward-breaking turns of phrase and little puppyish exclamations that concealed the bolting blood flow in his pants. Yes, men spoke a stench, but she hadn't smelled that particular sweet rotting top note of sex for a while now.

"How true, Dan." She cut in at an appropriate moment and gave him an effortless, medium-strength smile that allowed her to feel the air on her teeth. "And the reason for that is because we do basically the same thing, in a way. I'm just the photographic negative of the positive which is you."

"Exactly right," he said. "And by the way, is this what I have to look forward to in the future?"

"What's that?"

"You always staying a step ahead of me in conversation?"

"Does that bother you?"

"Not in the least," he said.

"Good, because the answer is yes."

He laughed his panting laugh. "You know what I wish about now?" he said.

"What's that?"

"That I didn't have to go to work."

"Well, then, call in sick," she said, knowing he wouldn't.

"I can't."

She mimed unhappiness, sticking out her lips.

"Yeah, I know," he said. "It's the last thing I want, either. But duty calls. And hey, I actually love my job. Are you laughing at me? It can happen to you, too."

"I'm not sure I ever really truly loved a job in my life," she said.

"Well, that's about to change," he said.

She looked at him carefully. "Yes," she said, and then, "How long will you be gone?"

"Till early afternoon, though if I can, I'll try to swing by before then. Can you deal with some time alone?"

"I'll manage."

"Remember, the drill is: no sudden movements if possible, lots of time lying down, and can you also call me regularly to check in? I could pop back in to say hi in as soon as two hours."

"Two hours," she said, her mind widening outward in a geographical sweep over the surrounding area.

"Yes, and Margot," he said, "I'm hoping and believing this is the start of something, but I'm not an idiot. Just like last night, the doors will be locked from the outside. I want you staying put."

A two-hour radius from Queens included at least four airports and twenty-five million people.

"Right," she said.

Another silence while he stared at her. She watched with relief as, having kept his head classically "turtled" in the protective lowering of the chin as a hedge against doubt, he now raised it up, exposing his neck. Just perceptibly there, she thought she saw his pulse beating.

"Chocolate bars in the right crisper drawer," he said, and winked. "Enjoy the house." And with that, leaning close, he brushed her lips with his again, but briefly this time, and then stood up and walked to the front door from where he turned, gave her an airy little wave that she pretended to catch openhanded and stuff in her pocket, and then pivoted away.

The door sighed shut behind him. Letting out the bottom half of a breath she'd been holding, she sat in perfect silence for a few minutes on the kitchen chair, as if waiting to see if this odd little house would do something, surprise her in some way. Then she got up, took a very hot shower, and slowly went through the drawers of the desk. In one of them she found a small metal box. This she battered slowly with a hammer she found in a utility drawer, smashing at it until it broke. In it were several candid outdoor photos of Dan France with a pretty woman, and as she hoped, a set of house keys. With these in hand, she dressed slowly, packed her bag and entered the small guest bathroom. She had already noted that unlike the other bathroom and the windows of the house, which were protected with frames of decorative wrought-iron bars, this small frosted window giving onto an alley was painted shut but otherwise unprotected. Retrieving a large screwdriver from the utility drawer, she slowly hammered the blade into the soft wood around the edges of the window until she was able to lever it open. Then, after lacing sneakers onto her feet, she gently leveraged herself off the toilet bowl tank and slithered through the enclosure. A soft, somewhat awkward landing on the cindery dirt, and she was standing up and dusting off her skirt and swapping the sneakers out for heels. She opened the back door with the key, retrieved her rolling bag, and as quickly as she was able, walked out of the shadowy little backyard and, unlatching the front gate, into the brilliant room of daylight waiting on the other side.

CHAPTER THIRTY-FIVE

Driving his mom's snorting, ancient car, he'd pulled up to the house—an indistinguishable pair of brick shoulders in an endless serried row of same—checked the address and then cut the engine. It was still dark out in Queens, though a violet glow was beginning in the east. Desperation made him calm, even if he wasn't in the least certain what he was going to do.

Potash had brought with him a small pair of field glasses, which dated from the period when his mother and father used to attend opera and ballet at Lincoln Center. He rolled down the windows. The night fragrance of sleeping trees poured into the car. The neighborhood was giving faint signs of awakening, with the squares of windows lighting up, and the occasional soft clacking of cutlery and dishes. Potash, underslept and overwhelmed, remembered well the deliciousness of lying as a child beneath the scratchy blanket at just this time of morning, with the day not yet hardened into the errands of the adult world and all of life still waiting in the soft, poured forms of the dawn.

But that was a thousand years ago. And that golden-limbed child had grown into a heavyhearted adult with a defect of mind that had let him be defrauded of that which was rightfully his. "Fighting for my frickin' life," he whispered to himself, unsheathing the field glasses from their case, "is what I'm doing." A big pane of light popped on in the house directly across the street. He had no need of field glasses to clearly discern a stocky figure in a T-shirt and jeans moving about a living room, setting things on a small table. The figure opened the fridge and stood a moment in the fall of yellow light, arm braced against the appliance, before withdrawing some items for breakfast. Even crooks have to eat. But was this in fact the crook, Potash wondered, or the cop that Berke had spoken of, or someone else?

After a moment, the man went away. Another small window lit up, and a couple of minutes later, the man returned, and continued to move around the room, making small adjustments and setting things out on the table. Potash watched, and as the rising sun began draining the undersea gloom from the scene, a woman walked slowly into the living room from stage left. She and the man chatted. Potash, now drawn entirely into the moment, slowly put the field glasses to his eyes. Across the sixty or so feet that separated him from her he discerned the telltale profile he'd never forget: proud nose, sensual lips, and hair that, though lightened and cropped, did not distract him from the truth: it was her.

Half unconsciously, he grunted as the impact of seeing Janelle hit him with a physical force. If he could have, he would have reached long arms across the street and throttled the neck she was now showing off as she smiled, swiveled her head and made morning conversation with her friend. He watched as she made those same winsome moves of the head with which she'd once lulled him into a defenseless trance, coquettishly dipping her face so that she could then look up at you from beneath the brake of the lashes, pursing her lips, dimpling her cheeks, flashing her green eyes and keeping herself, like a moving target, always fractionally ahead of where your gaze might light.

Then the man was leaning down to her, and as he kissed her a strange, mixed shock went through him—a feeling, oddly enough, of her humanity. But he would not allow it, and he closed his heart violently against the perception, muttering under his breath, "Motherfucker, I'm gonna get you."

By now, as the light of the street continued to lift, he felt exposed, sitting in the car with the small binoculars to his eyes, and so he quickly put them back in their case. Slumping downward, he began reading the paper in an attempt to render himself as inconspicuous as possible.

This was not the kind of neighborhood where people evidently worried about being spied upon. It was an area dense with families, and as if at a signal, within the next twenty minutes, doors began opening up all over and children spilled down the stairs and stoops, en route to school. Potash wasn't so far removed from his previous life to be unaffected by the spectacle of this orderly adherence to the dream of an education. Always, it was the disadvantaged, the marginal, the outcasts, who threw themselves at the opportunity. Chinese, Jamaicans, Dominicans, Kazakhstanis—over the years, how many times had he seen the arc of acculturation through the agency of a good public school turn a mumbling, socially awkward parent into a smooth exemplar of the American dream in a single generation? Rejects there were aplenty, but Potash, despite the mounting evidence of their gross inefficiency, was still proud of American schools.

But even as he let himself be buoyed a moment by these thoughts, he was recalled to the truth of his mission by the sight of the door of the house directly across the street opening and the man leaving.

He studied him closely a second. A thick, bullish neck sat atop an upper body expanded, probably, through weight lifting or contact sports. A cop haircut, boxed on the sides and long in front, crowned an undistinguished snub-nosed face. He wore a suit jacket, casually draped, and chinos finishing in cowboy boots. He didn't exactly hulk as he walked, but balletic he was not, swinging heavily into his car—the Range Rover, Potash noted—and starting it up.

He cut his eyes to the house. The woman was not visible. The Range Rover was pulling out and leaving the neighborhood. With a sudden rush of nerves, now that the moment was nearly upon him, he pondered his options. They were the following: call Berke, even though Berke had washed his hands of him. Call Cas, and wait for him to arrive in an explosion of ridiculousness and over-the-top verbiage; simply call the police and thereby have her questioned (but if the man who had just left was the police, then where would that leave him, Potash?); or do what he was deciding to do, which was to sit still and wait. He'd come this far, after all.

Several minutes went by in a state of furious confusion as he stared unseeing at the page of his newspaper, trying to figure out his next move. Eventually he decided that he'd simply take a walk around the block, clear his head and contemplate the possibilities; and he had actually placed his hand on the handle of the door, psyching himself up to leave the safety of the car, when his vision was arrested by something off to one side. It was her, the girl, opening the small gate of the house's fence and stepping with a certain tentative daintiness onto the driveway, a rolling cart behind her. Smoothly, without wasting any movement, he continued opening the car door, and then stood up and began walking toward her.

As he moved forward, he felt himself oddly tall, tippy on his feet. He noted that she was smiling absently, her eyes blinking rapidly, as if troubled by the morning sun. He walked directly toward her and planted himself in her path.

"Uh, yes?" she said, "Can I—?"

"Janelle, or whatever your name is, it's me," he said, unsmiling. "John Potash."

She continued to stare at him directly, silent.

"You really thought you'd get away with it, didn't you?"

She began beetling her brow.

"Do we know each other?" she said finally.

He gave a kind of sob of a laugh.

"Do we?" she repeated. "I'm thinking, based on your response, that maybe we do, in which case excuse me. Who do you think I am?"

Faintly, he was aware of the neighborhood all around him. Thronging with children fifteen minutes ago, it was now eerily silent. All the parents who had recently bid good-bye to their kids were now cleaning up, reading the papers, yet he knew it would take but a single scream to flood the street with concerned citizens.

"We can do this one of two ways," he said quietly. "Either you can restore the entirety of the money you embezzled from me, or you can go to jail."

"Embezzled? Jail?" Her brow beetled further. He was amazed to be this touchably close to the person who he had sought in dreams and fevered imaginings for ten whole days. A wavering white bracket seemed to be bristling in the air around him; he remembered, just in time, to breathe.

"Yes," he said, "jail time. That's what they give you when you steal, and when you steal a lot, as you did from me, and it was probably a hell of a lot more than that because who knows who else you stole from—" And here he stopped and looked at her in dawning disbelief. Because this somewhat pale, diminished version of the woman who'd ruined his life was now raising a sheaf of hair and showing him a terrible series of barred dots, a small ladder of bluish lines running in sequence on a shaved expanse of her skull while saying, quietly, "You can say whatever you want about me, but I'm recovering from a bad thing. I had a fall of some kind down the stairs, they tell me, and lost my memory." She shrugged her shoulders, emptily. "I'm sorry for what happened to you," she said. "It sounds awful."

The openness of his own throat and neck suddenly made him feel vulnerable. Was she somehow on the verge of wriggling away *again*? He pitched his voice as low as possible.

"I want you," he said, "to take me to whoever is responsible for you."

"I'm not sure who that is at the moment," she said calmly, and shrugged her shoulders again. "I just got out of rehab and if you wanna know the truth, I was taking a walk around the block."

"With a rolling bag?"

"To do a little shopping."

She looked at him, and for the first time he saw a faint flicker of something like recognition, a briefest of ripples in the smooth, calm shining of her green eyes.

"Okay, here's what we're gonna do," he said. "We're gonna go indoors and you're either gonna phone your bank and tell them we're coming by to pick up an awfully big cashier's check, or wire transfer the money back into mine through the computer, and once I see that it's back in my account, I won't press felony charges, and that's it. Felony charges," he repeated.

But despite everything, he heard the reasonableness of his reconciliator's tone, leaving his mouth eager to find common ground, and pitching his voice deliberately lower, he repeated, "Do you hear me?"

She was looking past him and smiling. Potash irritably swiveled his head. A neighbor, walking his dog, was waving at her cheerfully.

"Either I get satisfaction," he said in the same voice, "or this whole neighborhood is going to know the truth about you in about thirty seconds."

"Mr.?" she said.

"John Potash."

"Yes. Clearly, you're very upset. Something bad was done to you. Of that I have no doubt. But really"—and here she shook her head and made a face as if appealing to some invisible witness—"what do you want me to do?"

"Six hundred and fifty thousand dollars," he said, "of my money, and my elderly mother's money and my wife's money."

She put her hand on her breast. He recognized the gesture.

"That's horrible!"

"Thanks for the sympathy. You've got five minutes."

"Mr. Potash," she said in that same somewhat slowed-down version of the voice he once knew; the same timbre, but ghosted now in the apparent aftermath of that surgery whose blue lines crisscrossed her skull, "you seem like a nice person. I'd like to try to help you. But . . ."

Now, more than ever, he wished for Berke. Berke would have known exactly what to do. But the vast universe of police procedure with its certainties and end-stopped threats floated, maddeningly, just a few feet out of reach.

"I am not leaving," he said, "until I get satisfaction." He raised his cell phone. "And I'm perfectly happy to call the local police department and explain to them that a known criminal happens to living at 5775 Ocean Boulevard and see how they feel about that."

She was nodding her head, the gesture located somewhere between sympathy and pity.

"If I were in your shoes," she said, "I'm sure I'd do the exact same thing."

She stopped nodding her head and looked him directly in the eyes. He felt a peculiar current of energy tingling down the backs of his legs. Without being exactly aware of what he was doing, he dwelled on the pleasure it would give him to smash her skull.

"I'll tell you what," she said, as if the idea had just occurred to her. "Why don't I take you back inside the house, and if you can show me this terrible thing that happened to your accounts on the computer, maybe I can try to help or call someone who can?"

"We'll go into the house," said Potash, masterfully dissimulating the surge of violence, "and we'll look up our accounts on the computer, mine and yours, and then you'll pay me back, and if it's not all the money, to the very last dime, I'll call the cops."

"Mr. Potash—John, these threats of yours, they don't do anything to me, don't you see? Now be reasonable and follow me inside, please."

He said nothing, but kept close behind her as she backtracked toward the house. Despite the tension of the moment, he couldn't help but note that her face seemed shrunken and gray and that she walked more haltingly than he remembered, with less of that smooth, butt-driven saunter that advertised "sexual power here." Something bad, it was clear, had happened to her. Possibly some other aggrieved party had gotten to her first. But he wouldn't dwell on it. He was here on a one-pointed mission of his own.

She turned around and touched him on the sleeve and he yanked his arm back as if snakebit. She recoiled a moment in surprise.

"I only wanted to tell you that for security, we keep the front door locked so I'm going to go around back to let myself in. Would you like to accompany me?"

He wouldn't dignify her question with a response, but stayed right behind her as they crossed the yard, she opened the gate and they proceeded through to the small somewhat sunless backyard and up a flight of three brick steps.

"This is a little odd," she said, putting a key in the lock and squinting while doing so with the evident effort of coordination, "that I'm letting a man I don't know into the house. But hey"—she shrugged her shoulders again—"you have a trustworthy face." She smiled at him for the first time. "I used to be a connoisseur of faces."

But Potash refused, again, to acknowledge the comment and merely made a directional nod to push her attention back to the lock. She turned the key and he followed her inside the house.

Dark-wood walls, a faint sour smell of furniture polish and a warm overlay of cooking. She brought him through the sunny kitchen, still redolent of breakfast, and into an adjoining study where a laptop lay on a desk.

"Computer," she said simply. Bending over it, she opened the case and booted it up. It pinged loudly, and they both started. "Okay?" she said.

"Mmm," Potash said, noncommittal.

She was bent over the keyboard, still standing, while with light, deft taps of the fingers she punched in her user name and password, when Potash's phone trilled. He was going to ignore it, but on instinct, allowed himself a peek. It was his mother, he saw.

Any other time, he would have let it ring through. But this was the morning of her first day home from the hospital, and the mortality-flavor of the moment was uppermost in his mind.

Keeping his eyes riveted on the screen, he moved the phone carefully to his ear.

"Mom?"

"Where are you?" was her hello.

"I'm not far, Mom, and should be home soon. How are you, and how"—he slipped the card of the home health aide out of his pocket—"is Luz?"

"Luz has no idea of what the word 'poached' is. Can you imagine?"

Potash, despite the gravity of the moment, had to smile.

"Mom," he said, "if poached eggs are the only problem you're having, then I know that things can't be that bad overall."

"There you're wrong," said his mother, but he could hear the smile in her voice as well.

The *New York Times* page had now appeared on the screen. Margot was punching numbers rapidly, and the Chase Manhattan home page appeared. She input her user name and password and hit the log-in.

"John," his mother was saying, "it's a good morning to be alive. Your brother is coming over soon, and it would be wonderful if you were here as well, instead of running off on some crazy early morning errand. Where are you again, dear?"

Margot was standing up and inclining her head toward the open door of the nearby bathroom, her index finger raised as in "one minute."

The rolling bag was parked at his feet. It was 8:21 in the morning. Potash nodded gravely.

"At someone's house on an errand," he said. "I won't be long."

Margot clopped the ten feet down the hall and shut the door. Potash bent toward the screen.

"You know," his mother said, "ever since my little stay in the hospital I feel like all I wanna do is spend time with my sons."

A fresh wave of guilt for his move to California crashed over him, but he said only, "I think your sons feel the same way, Mom. For my part, I've gotta head back to Calfornia tomorrow, but I'll be returning soon. I mean really soon. And there's always the phone."

"Yes," she said, as he pressed the onscreen button for "checking." The hall toilet flushed. "There is always that," she added. There was then a silence on the phone, interrupted, faintly, by a barrage of broken, fluting English such as that spoken by a native Spanish-language speaker.

"No," he heard his mother say, "in the water, Miss, in the hot water," and then in a tone of exasperated confidence, to Potash: "Can I tell you something?" He thought he knew what was coming but said obligingly, "What?"

"I just hate having strangers in the house, that's all."

"It's only temporary, Mom."

"Is it? But how can you be sure?"

"Because you're going to get better, is how."

Now they were on familiar ground. Potash had already discovered that he was incapable of admitting Death into the picture. Perhaps this was why he'd married a woman whose radiant positivity seemed to outshine his own morbid inclinations. "You're slowly going to get your strength back, Mom," he said, "and then you're going to outlive all of us!"

This was the same phrase he'd used in his father's declining years. It was as threadbare as the old T-shirts of his father's, worn nearly to transparency. But he couldn't help himself.

"Come home, John," she said in a soft voice.

"I will," he said, and then a rush of alertness at the extended silence around him in the house prickled the hairs on the back of his neck. "Mom, I gotta go!" he said, and hung up on her in the middle of gabbing something indignant, and trotted the few steps down the hall to the bathroom door.

"Margot," he said loudly. The silence that met his utterance was like swallowing something cold and feeling it go slowly all the way down.

"Margot?" He rattled the handle of the door, and then called her name louder, "Margot?"

In the ongoing silence, the wave of rage that had been idling offshore for days suddenly stood up and swept forward. Lowering his head, he backed up a few feet and with a running start and putting his shoulder into it, smashed the thin pine door right off its hinges.

The bathroom was empty. The tiles and the tub were spotless, but on one wall, the window had been jimmied open. Potash, sinking to his knees in the antiseptic white confines that smelled faintly of citrus and the bracing terpenes of shower products, began brokenly to weep.

CHAPTER THIRTY-SIX

Glynis's arrival home was preceded by a lone e-mail that in its entirety read, "I'm returning tomorrow."

Having passed an anxious twenty-four hours unsuccessfully disguised to himself as a husband with nothing particular on his mind, Lawrence was sitting reading in the living room the next afternoon when he heard the low chuckle of the key in the lock. He shot to his feet, unnecessarily brushing lint off his pantlegs as he crossed the living room floor. But before he could get to the door she had opened it and taken a step forward into the room, her travel bag behind her.

"Hi," she said calmly.

"Glyn." He reached forward to hug her, but she only partially accepted the embrace, stiffening while he clasped her to him and then pulling back to pivot slowly in place while saying, "Wow, the place looks . . . nice."

"It should look nice. I worked at it."

"I can tell."

She'd been gone only five days and yet she was more put-together, sharper, more composed than he expected. Clearly she hadn't passed her time—as on the previous two marital furloughs—shedding tears.

"You bought flowers?" she said.

"Yes, jonquils."

"I'm touched, and migod, the windows too?"

"That's right," he was nodding, "and the crawl space as well."

"*The crawl space?* What's got into you, Lawrence?"

"Hey, I had to do something." He smiled as he shrugged his shoulders. "A hundred years ago I might have torn my garments. In this case, I just cleaned the place."

"I should go away more often," she said, and laughed.

"And you?" he asked.

"Me?"

"What penance did *you* perform?"

He was trying for humor himself, but she only peered through the window out at the garden a long moment and said, "God, there's nothing like being away to help remember how lovely this house is."

"Yes," he said.

She swiveled her face slowly back to his. After his last "slippage" of many years earlier, they'd seen a marriage counselor who had spoken of the need for "individuation" in the partners in a long-term marriage. Psychic unity, if it was to survive, apparently needed regular breaks of breathing room. But all he wanted, passionately at the moment, was to kiss and hug her.

"What did I do?" she asked. "Well, Marley is a wonderful woman, but she runs with a pretty fast crowd."

"So I gather," he said. "And you ran along with them?"

"After a fashion," she said.

"What's that mean?"

"Lawrence?"

"Yes, Glyn."

"This is not the time for that conversation."

"Right. Would you like something, a tea or anything?" he asked.

"No, I'm fine."

He felt vaguely a fool for having overshot the natural rhythm of their chat, but she was smiling at him.

"You didn't notice," she said.

"Didn't notice . . . what?"

She touched her hair and he saw it had been cut and highlighted.

"Of course!" he cried, with overemphasis. "And it looks lovely."

"Do you think so? I was afraid it was too short."

"No, not at all. It makes you look . . . French?"

"Like those dancers we saw at the Crazy Horse club in Paris."

"Well, you do have the legs for it," he said, laughing.

"Did you see the girl while I was gone?"

The words seemed to explode in the air off the side of his head and momentarily deafen him. Slowly he put his hands up on either side of his head and held them there, as if measuring the size of his surprise.

"Okay, let's begin with this, first," he said in his professionally calm voice. "The first thing is, you're entitled to be disappointed in me. I understand that now and want you to know. What I did was a silly, stupid no-account thing at bottom, but of course you're sensitive after our . . . past."

"But did you?"

"What?"

"See the girl."

He dropped his hands back to his sides. Alone in the two days since his dinner with Margot, he'd decided that when this moment came, he would lie about it, as repugnant as that was to him. He would lie about it because to explain what he'd done would be impossible.

"Of course not."

"I see."

"But I can assure you," he said, "that she won't be a problem in our lives anymore."

"I thought you said you didn't see her."

"I didn't."

"Then what are you talking about?"

"Glynis."

"Yes."

"Relax."

"I'm just saying you seem awfully sure about the fate of someone you've had nothing to do with."

"Do we really want to do this?" he asked, "now, the very first moment you're back?"

But instead of responding directly, she cast her eyes in another circuit around the house.

"Thanks for keeping everything so tidy while I was away," she said, leaving Lawrence with the feeling they'd been slammed, infuriatingly, all the way back to exactly where they'd been before she'd left. She was regarding him for a moment with a faint, indecipherable smile, and then she turned and walked up the stairs with her cart bumping after her. Though he wanted to, he knew better than to call her back.

That night, he cooked chicken Djibouti. Having perfected it in her absence, he adjusted the spice mix to a milder heat for her, and from a culinary point of view it went over wonderfully. But the exotic entrée seemed only to underline their domestic disconnect.

In the past, after spats, they had often taxied along commonplaces for a few hours or a day before lifting back up into the air of their accustomed affection for each other. But on this night their marriage felt to Lawrence like a frightened animal, a humpbacked, hissing cat stuck in a tree.

In bed afterward, she was friendly but somewhat distant. Lovemaking, which especially since their retreat of sexual yoga he believed the ultimate reboot of a relationship, was now clearly off-limits. But even sleeping next to her under the circumstances felt restorative and a small step toward eventual reconciliation. The next morning he was up early, determined to have a good day.

Dotingly, he served her breakfast in bed, having made her pancakes with blueberries drenched in maple syrup. She was touched by the gesture, and though they hadn't made love, the house itself, the warm, accustomed routines and the sheer beauty of the surroundings were working on her, he could tell. Her face was plumped and smooth from a good night's sleep and she reached out while they ate and touched his hand with hers and kept it there. They would have a bracingly candid conversation soon, he was sure, and be that much closer to a return to the fullness of previous.

As to the question, What had finally happened with the girl—well, what did it matter? He kissed his wife's hand and then got up to make her a coffee. Five minutes later, Lawrence was clumping back out to the breakfast nook in his Crocs, steaming cup in hand, bending forward in the relieved certainty of being at last back on solid ground.

CHAPTER THIRTY-SEVEN

As soon as she hit the dirt outside the bathroom window, she ran as fast as she could to the nearest cross street, where she almost immediately caught a cab. She gave the driver directions and shut her eyes against the sick, spilling feeling in her head while the car seemed to leap, light as a locust, across the Queensboro Bridge and into Midtown Manhattan.

She asked the cabbie to stop at a store where she could buy a small rolling bag. Not long after, the cab was pulling up to her destination near Herald Square. She got out gingerly, the chased bronze doors of the bank opened before her like two tall sentries, and she stepped into an elevator that drew her swiftly upward. The sudden shift of altitude worsened her queasiness, but she recovered in time to step out of the elevator as it hissed open and present her credentials to the woman at the desk. She was then escorted by a man wearing an official blue blazer of a sort to a room bare save for a green lamp on a heavy lacquered wooden table. She sat down and folded her hands on the table, waiting until the man returned and placed before her the grey rectangular shape of her safety-deposit box.

The night before, lying in bed in Dan France's house after dinner, she'd watched as a starburst of recollection, widening outward, slowly lit up a landscape of memory. Down the center of that memory there poured a small river, carrying her attention forward. The water wrinkled a little bit as it picked up speed along the widening part of the river and then it gathered mass and power as it poured off an outcropping and fell thundering against the truth.

The truth was now sitting two feet from her face. Reaching forward and opening the safety-deposit box, she found what she was looking for: more than a million dollars in nontraceable Guatemalan government bearer's bonds, redeemable at nearly any bank in the world, along with a credit card, a phone, and a passport. The sound wrenched from her diaphragm was a feral moan of joy.

At her request, the cab had remained waiting downstairs. With the contents of the safety-deposit box zipped securely into her rolling bag, she asked the driver, a Sikh by the name of Jai Dev, to head straight to Kennedy Airport. He zoomed away with a speed that gave her that nauseous feeling in her head again, and she rapped on the partition, telling him to slow down, and then sank back into her seat, and braced a hand over her eyes. In her head was a branching candelabra of European cities inhabited by clusters of the black-clad girlfriends from college, with whom occasionally she was still in touch. Successfully transplanted, they were now bringing up children in foreign languages. Beyond them, vast, beautiful belts of beachside homes striped the coasts of islands in the chain of the Dutch Antilles and the British Virgin Islands, where wealthy men had once upon a time flown her for extended dalliances. Somewhere, in one of those places, or at least a dozen others, a special, unmolested peace was waiting. The soft pull of that peace was already in the air and coming toward her. It was sized to fit her exactly and tricked out with all the correct details. The future and the past were connected by an infinitely long string, and as one yanked shut, the other slammed open.

And then, not long after, they were pulling up to the airport.

CHAPTER THIRTY-EIGHT

The whole ride back to California from New York on the red-eye, Potash was unable to sleep, and awake in the dark, he found himself screening sad confessional scenarios in his head. He saw his wife and himself on a bluff overlooking the Pacific, with the harp-shaped waves hissing, and the birds screaming, while they held hands across a tablecloth strewn with figs, prosciutto, and baguette crusts, and he whispered the words. "Honey, we're broke." Or facing each other over a glass of wine, in a restaurant with long views of vineyards, as he gave a winsome smile, preemptively summoning tenderness from her, before saying, "I'm afraid I've got something to tell you."

And watched as the light died slowly away from her face.

A rich literature existed of the impact of sudden bankruptcy on marriages. Potash, as he ate his inflight meal of stringy beef and lukewarm rice, mentally reviewed the literature. He knew that the statistics gave him only a 50 percent chance of getting through the upcoming months, undivorced. He knew that educated opinion concurred nearly unanimously on the gravity of the situation. And he knew as well that one educated opinion in particular begged to differ. The day before, when he returned to her house from his futile mission in Queens, his mother had never looked frailer, nor more transparent, nor more already halfway to the next world. But that didn't stop her from greeting him with the verbal equivalent of a shot across the bow.

"Money," she said flatly, as he stood in the doorway.

"Money?" asked Potash, who having first canvassed Margot's neighborhood on foot and then fruitlessly in his car, now had a headache beginning at the very base of his spine.

"Yes, money," she said. "I'm here to tell you it doesn't matter."

He made a sound somewhere between a cough and a groan.

"Seriously, John. What happened in the hospital made one thing veeeery clear. You, son, are lucky."

She patted the couch next to her for him to sit down.

"Lucky," he said, crossing the room and lowering himself slowly down to the cushions, "is not how I feel at the moment."

She smiled at him coquettishly. "You're lucky because you have true love, John. And how many people have that, ever? Do you think your father and I had that? No, we did not."

"This is all very nice to hear, but really—"

"Romance"—she looked over his head and into the middle distance where the ancient memories were stored—"wasn't on the menu for Dad and me. Oh, a little bit maybe, at the very beginning. After all, there's got to be some reason to get together. But life swept in pretty quickly and put out those flames, oh yes it did. A stern teacher, life. And it keeps repeating the same lessons till you cry uncle."

"Mom," he said.

Tremendously canny, she fixed him with her smoky green eyes.

"A brightness has gone from the world," she said, "and I don't think that's just me being old. Look around. The wars, the bad faith, the sense of menace like a disease—I'm happy I'm not a young person today. But you've got a great marriage, John. That's my point. A marriage like that you don't walk away from just because you lost your dough. Especially in this day and age."

"Thank you," he said miserably, "for the advice."

"You're welcome." She sat back up straight. "And now, if you don't mind me butting in, you should call her and tell her everything."

"*What?*" he cried.

"Yes." She was nodding in that same knowing way that had dependably infuriated him as a child. "She'll be hurt, she'll be disappointed, maybe she'll cry. No, she *will* cry, poor thing. Anabella's like that. She feels things strongly. But then she'll get over it."

"Are you really," he said in a voice of suppressed fury, "telling me what to do with my own wife?"

"And why not?" She shrugged, utterly indifferent to his anger.

His mother was eighty-seven years old. In a familiar movement of feeling, he drew the displeasure at her down, down, through the bottommost point of his belly, where it dissolved as warmth. Then he looked up, put his hands on the pointy twists of her shoulders where the bones ended, and with a certain difficulty, smiled.

"Maybe you're right," he said.

"No, I *am* right."

"Well, there's no denying I screwed up royally, that's for sure."

"Who hasn't? What's important is what you do now, post-mess, John."

"Agreed," he said.

"Good," she said. But this last bit of jaunty buoyancy with her eldest son had evidently cost her, because she suddenly made a small, sour crimp of the lips as if tasting bad food, and her eyelids lowered over her eyes. After a moment of panic, he realized that she had simply fallen asleep.

The warping sound of the jet engines changed pitch, and Potash, waking up out of a fitful sleep as they began making their descent to San Francisco International Airport, girded himself afresh. He never had made that call to Anabella, and his reckoning with her still lay a few hours ahead of him. Meanwhile they were dropping through the immensity of dawn skies toward the tiny strip of runway, and not long after, he was exiting the plane into the slightly more humid, saturated air of the West Coast. He passed through the security checkpoint back into the concourse where a row of drivers with shakily lettered signs held at their chests stood as if posing for mug shots. His step quickening, he was about to get on the mobile walkway to the parking garage when he suddenly stopped, amazed. About fifty feet away, unseeing, her head inclined into a cell phone, was his wife.

"Anabella?" he yelled, but in the roaring concourse she couldn't hear him. He began walking rapidly toward her, smiling despite everything because, bankruptcy or no, the sight of her fresh, familiar face in the chilly anonymity of the airport gave him a charge of pleasure. But when she raised her eyes to his she communicated to him a bolt of such sincere sadness that it actually caused his stride to falter as he drew up to her, kissed her quickly on the lips, and then pulled back, brow furrowing, his hands on her elbows.

"But what are you—?"

"Not good," she interrupted him. And then in a hoarse voice, "Oh, I wish I wasn't here for this, but your mother died, John. Not long after you left, apparently. Sweetheart, I'm just so sorry."

The grief arrived instantly, centered in his body. While his mind was still processing the conversation, his abdomen had already clenched tight and begun driving hard, racking sobs through his throat. These continued violently as his wife held him and repeated his name, kissing his ears and neck. When the worst of the first flurry had passed, she gave him a clump of tissues, and then led him by the hand—even in extremis, she was organized—to the conveniently nearby airport chapel. After the frenzy of the terminal, the silence of the small, dim carpeted space was absolute. Potash felt himself floating rather than walking over to a nearby riser. They sat down, holding hands, and she began to speak.

"This isn't only a sad moment," she said softly, "and I want you to remember that over the next days, John. Your mother left life on her own terms. She knew exactly what she was doing until the very end, and she did it all without pain. The home health aide was very moved. There is such a thing as a good death, and she had one. Really, she left like a goddess." She began to cry herself. "She was a fierce, very special person, and I'll miss her."

Through his chest, which had about it the dull ache of extended shouting, Potash felt the fresh charge of his tears massing, and shut his eyes. He'd been dreading this moment since that afternoon, age nine, when he'd looked out the window of his suburban home and first seen death already stalking the bright insignias of daylight— home, parents, cars, the world. All of that, down to its very last fizzing atoms, would one day go away. Yet now that it had come to pass, his first perception was that the death of his mother was not only sad but weirdly *roomy* somehow. There was space there. Massaging his neck, touching his ears and temples, his wife was pulling him closer, whispering something consoling. But what was consoling him at that moment was only partly the familiar drawling tones of her voice. He was also thinking that in the Bardo or interspace where the recently dead souls loitered while nostalgically looking back over the landscape of their works and days, his mother was not only serene, but probably happy as well. Her role in life, below that sense she gave him of always being in burden to an obscure sorrow, was to protect him from his own foolishness. And wherever she was in her passage to the next world, she was certainly taking satisfaction from the fact that she'd done it yet again. The sale of her house would entirely make up for the loss of his savings.

"Dear Lord," said Potash, wanting his mother to know this, praying in some way that she did. Did the soul ever grow older? That nine-year-old boy was still looking out of his eyes. Life was deeper, more punishing, more deliciously fraught than that child could have ever imagined, and filled with redemptions in the least likely of places. The towering wave of tears was about to fall, but there was still time for him to bury his face in the fragrant glen of his wife's neck, and mutter the words "Thank you" out loud. Even better, in the quiet space of the chapel, in the moment before the rest of his life began, there was still time to mean them.

CHAPTER THIRTY-NINE

"We lie to our spouses, our bosses, our friends, and to ourselves most of all." Lawrence stared out at the dark, spreading sea of faces and drew a tired breath. "Lying," he said, "is human nature, alas. It's as hardwired into us as the gag reflex or the contraction of the pupils of your eyes in bright light."

There was the familiar soft fluttering of laptop keyboards and of pens scratching paper in the dark.

"The truth, my friends, is that, despite all our so-called psychological sophistication, there still are no hard and fast markers to determine whether or not another person is telling the truth. What we do know," Lawrence said, "is that the lie cuts you off forever from its recipient. It walls you off in the alternate universe of your falsehood, and whoever you've just lied to is a little farther away from you than they were before, and as often as not stuck there permanently. Is this clear?"

He paused. He was breathing hard. Differently from before, he now tended to get exercised on the podium, working himself up, and occasionally, when the mood took him, defensively reeling off lists of statistics. His wife had suggested yoga. He'd begun taking Ativan, nights.

He cleared his throat. " 'Every violation of truth is a sort of suicide,' said a great American named Ralph Waldo Emerson. But he didn't mean that literally, of course." He paused. "Or did he?"

He'd spotted her the day before, and though he'd tried, per his new arrangement with himself, to look away, those shining eyes, now picked out of the darkness on his far left, caused a Bump, and no mistake about it. Slowly, for the first time since she'd arrived, she raised her hand.

"Yes, Miss . . ."

"Livia," she said. Incapable of not noticing, he espied a pair of full breasts, levered into prominence by the action of her raising her arm.

"I think the full quote," she said, shutting her eyes, "is 'Every violation of truth is not only a sort of *suicide* in the liar, but is a stab at the health of human society.' " The eyes flew open, triumphant. "I'm doing my thesis on Emerson," she said by way of explanation, smiling.

Lawrence was nodding up and down and applauding with small taps of his hands. "Very good, Livia," he said softly. "No, I mean *very* good."

His BlackBerry buzzed. Normally he placed it on silent, but he must have forgotten and set it to vibrate. He ignored it.

"Our culture is running scared," he said, looking out over the room and doing his best to avoid the girl's shining face, which had now positioned itself for that beautiful airborne game of catch and volley of glances he knew so well. "Scared," he said, "in part because of the plague of falsehoods afflicting us from the ground up. Did you know that styles of lying have what academics call a gender bias? That women lie more often to make someone feel good and men to make someone *look* good?" A hum, detaching itself from the audience, rose into the air of the hall. "That high school kids from nonreligious schools cheat significantly less than their more religious counterparts? Or that ninety-five percent of college students say they would lie to get a job."

His BlackBerry buzzed again and then pinged with a text. He pulled it out, saw that both the call and message were from his wife, and slid it back in his pocket. Ever since what they both referred to as the "crisis," they'd grown newly delicate and attentive to each other, and the frantic makeup sex which had followed upon her return from Marley had recovered its calm, custodial twice-monthly frequency. Sometimes he felt that, post-crisis, they were watching themselves enact idealized versions of their own lives, a little bit like a couple writing letters to each other while sitting at the dinner table.

"I wanna shift gears," he said, "to the demo phase of things. In this phase we'll be getting up close and personal with that part of our body which has the densest, deepest quantity of readable details of all: the human face. To do that we're gonna need a volunteer from the audience." A crop of hands shot up, among them Livia's. He deliberately swiveled his attention from her and chose a heavy-set woman with chopped blond hair.

"You, please, if you don't mind."

Gratified, the woman got to her feet and began making her way effortlessly down the central aisle to the small raised stage. She was drawing near when in the darkness of the back of the room a door opened, letting in light. Into that light stepped a uniformed policeman and a man in a dark suit jacket and tie.

Lawrence's chest was suddenly invaded by a sensation of intense cold. As calmly as he could, he cleared his throat and held out one hand, traffic-cop style. "Miss," he said to the woman about to mount the stage, "would you please return to your seat? Let's take a ten-minute break, and then we'll get right back to it."

The two men were standing silent at the back of the small theater, carefully studying Lawrence. The audience members, who would have normally been already heading to the nearby cafeteria, remained glued to their seats, making a low, excited murmur of conversation. Lawrence understood exactly why the cops were there. In some strange way, he'd been waiting for them from the moment he'd heard the thick, deep thunks of Margot's head hitting the stairs as she fell. Over the days and weeks since, his many kindnesses and small acts of marital loyalty had been at least in part propitiatory. They'd been addressed to these men and others like them in the hope that they might collectively see his goodness of heart and desist from their pursuit. But it hadn't worked.

Lawrence drew a deep breath and made a tunnel in front of his eyes. He knew that people were a marble of malice and generosity, and that all the good intentions in the world couldn't pry them open when they'd been sealed shut by childhood trauma, and wishing with all one's might couldn't turn a bad person into a good. On the small stage of its life span, the human animal pretended to know its own nature; this was its special charge, its species destiny. Twenty-five years ago, he'd hit the man. The man had banged his head on the ground. Two months ago, after having kept that impulse under wraps for all that intervening time, he'd repeated the violence. Below everything humankind could do to make of it an orderly place, life was still a lottery where goodness wasn't even minimally a precondition of success. His fate, however, had been to pick a winning ticket, hadn't it? In the larger scheme of things, definitely. He loved his wife, who seemed suddenly islanded in a sunny, carefree place that was rapidly receding out of sight into his future. It was presently a dot so small he could barely see it anymore. The cops in the back of the room were looking at him levelly. Their gaze communicated both the gravity of the situation and their shared desire to avoid a scene. The tunnel in front of his eyes was holding steady. He raised his head, threw back his shoulders, and walked into it.

CHAPTER FORTY

The cab deposited her at Kennedy airport. Somewhere, people alerted to her absence were probably already hunting through her clothes, searching her documents and accounts in an effort to box her in, track her down. She ignored that and got slowly out of the car, giving Jai Dev a tip that left him muttering with disbelieving joy. Then she steadied herself on the handle of her rolling bag, proceeded through the sliding glass doors into the terminal and froze, unable to walk any farther.

The main concourse gave the impression of shooting away from her in every direction. People were surging forward with blind directional intensity, deafened by the yelling faces of clocks and titanically amplified voices and bells ringing without obvious purpose and the space itself, which seemed to roar continuously. Through this space poured faces, an endless sea of features rushing by at eye level.

In the quiet weeks of hospital and rehab, she had been pampered. The faces she'd seen there were usually curled subtly in concern for her: the underthrust lower lip, the slight downturn of the eyes. But here she saw her fellow citizens of the world streaming by her plain, and the truth shocked. These faces were ugly, stranded by inner lives grown old too quickly or too slowly; pasty with ill-health, or drawn back in a snarl of appetite on the bones and left to harden there. To these add the many round, soft faces of the American Midwest, fattened on grains and beef, along with crooking lean country faces of inbred cleverness, and young girls dimpling and quick across the eyes and cheeks. The elderly, covered with a dust of age, carried pleated expressions around like disused table linen or drapes. And everywhere, she thought, was the question, What final truth do I represent? What vision, what original mystery do I uphold? Eyes filled with gel to refract light; teeth in the mouths to grind animals and plants to nutritious paste, and brains to pity the disappearing planet: she looked at the huge, stutter-step pour of humanity with confusion, and slumped against the metal edge of a newsstand, waiting till the dizziness, the strange negative rapture, had passed.

When she felt able to, she pushed away from the newsstand, walked slowly to the United counter, bought a ticket, and headed for the gate. Security made her laugh, it seemed so mechanical and stupid compared to the subtler onboard weapon of human insight. Having passed through the metal detector, she gathered her belongings, but instead of replacing her cell phone, placed it in her outer pocket and entered the nearby bathroom.

In the neutral fluorescent light, she found a stall and sat clothed on the toilet. The face of the cell phone when she withdrew it from her pocket looked to her like a woman with her mouth open, screaming. She wouldn't miss it where she was going, she thought, pulling the battery out, and then flushing it piece by piece down the toilet. And she wouldn't make the mistake of being geo-tracked and traced.

Life was an endless process of shedding skins, and she was the cobra that suns itself on a rock.

Back at her gate, after a wait of another hour or so, they began to board the plane. Dimly she was aware of hunger. Vaguely she was conscious of those odd pinging and bridling sick feelings along her skin that had been coming and going all day. But she ignored them, and concentrated on heading down a boarding ramp ribbed like a gullet. It wasn't till she was about to enter the plane that she realized how thready, loose, dirty everything was around her. The white of the plane was streaked with rivulets of gray grime. The big door had tiny coronas of rust around the bolts. In her mind, preparing for this moment over the previous day, she'd imagined the jet as an immaculate capsule traveling through heavenly regions of space before setting down in a new destination, but all it was, she now saw, was a kind of tired old bus.

She boarded, stowed her bag, took her window seat, placed her hands between her knees, and pressed hard, trying to make the nausea go away. A few minutes later, the aisle seat was taken by a man. Out of the sides of her eyes, she watched him sit down, retrieve the inflight magazine and begin paging through it. She shut her eyes and then opened them slowly, preparing herself.

"Excuse me," she said, and when he turned to her she beheld an attractive fortysomething face, filled with easy symmetries.

"Do you know how long the flight is supposed to be?"

"Nine hours," he said, and while he smiled she found her eyes ticking over him in that swift, inventorying way that had once been second nature: the suit jacket, beautifully cut; the hair, with the suave joinery of something expensive; the shirt, tieless and open on a chest filled with matted hair. Businessman. Possibly Jewish. Sexual and no ring.

"Wow," she said.

"Longer than you expected?"

"Much."

"*Better settle in.*"

"*Definitely.*"

With a roar, the plane ran headlong down the runway and flung itself into the air. She continued to watch him paging through a magazine with the light, lifted concentration of a man waiting for the opportunity to speak. Already a mile below, and shooting away beneath the tail, the earth with its crazy schemes, its dupes, its dead parents, and its long, bloody histories of right and wrong, was dwindling away to nothingness, a memory, a wisp, a forgotten breath.

"*We're expecting turbulence,*" *the man said, a finger hovering over a page.*

"*Where'd you hear that?*"

"*The captain, chatting with an attendant.*"

A calm, measured-sounding, mid-Atlantic voice, with the slightly adenoidal twinge of motherlove often found in firstborn sons.

"*Yikes,*" *she said.*

"*I know.*" *He grinned.*

They each returned to their magazines. The plane climbed and climbed. It reached upward like someone trying to win a prize. When they finally rose through the last levels of cloud and into the permanent, brilliant high-altitude sun, arriving from millions of miles away to make her comfortable this very minute, she put away the magazine. He was watching her out of the corner of his eyes, she understood. His face had the large overlip of someone in love with stimulation and the expansive nostrils of a person born generous. She yawned, covering her mouth.

She owed men everything and nothing. Lawrence Billings was probably about to get arrested at any minute and feeling sick to his soul. Her father was rotting to a kind of shredded tobacco underground. Mr. Wilkington the English teacher was long dead with all his tuneful poetry gone with him, and Clive Pemberthy was no doubt sleeping off his latest conquest en route to an early heart attack. In memory, they continued trooping across her vision, a solemn procession of boys and then men, each of them taking his turn and passionately pleading his case. Many of them were married. These were invariably the most winsome in their appeal. Though he'd stopped reading, the man next to her was continuing to stare frozenly at the page.

She settled back into her seat, steepled her fingers together, rested her chin on them, and turned on him a tidy little smile. Irresistibly, his face slid sideways before his eyes flared and settled on hers. Men spoke a stench. She sniffed delicately.

"So," she said.

ACKNOWLEDGMENTS

To my agent, Betsy Lerner, who was midwife, sharpshooter, all-weather genius, and steadfast friend on this book; to Enrico Perotti, Stephen O'Shea, Carlo Pizzati, Bruce Ettinger, Peter Cole, Mark Kamine, great readers all; to Susan Aposhyan, Martin Earl, Brian Kitely, Kip Hunter, Nevine Michaan, Tracey Alexander, Susan Bell, Don Berger, and Lars Skogen for varying forms of hospitality and wisdom; to the fabulous Dana Prescott of Civitella Ranieri; to Kirk Ruth, Ed Hernstadt, and Carrie Cohen of the U.S. District Attorney's Office, Southern District of New York, for technical support; to the crack crew of wizards at William Morrow, Henry Ferris, Tavia Kowalchuk, and Andy Dodds; to my beautiful pair of stepsons, Noah and Eli, and finally to the woman whose radiance, forbearance and abiding love lit every step of the way of this book and of the life that went into it, Judy Godec—thank you from the heart.